Lorraine Lucas
Box 120
16530 Tazewell St.
Saint Paul, VA 24283-3614

ANGELS
IN THE
SNOW

ANGELS
IN THE
SNOW

— A Novella —

MELODY CARLSON

Fleming H. Revell
A Division of Baker Book House Co
Grand Rapids, Michigan 49516

Published by Fleming H. Revell
a division of Baker Book House Company
P.O. Box 6287, Grand Rapids, MI 49516-6287

Printed in the United States of America

ISBN 0-8007-1816-X

1

The isolation felt complete now. Snowflakes tumbled non-stop from a pewter sky, silently encompassing her like a living, moving fortress. Claire experienced a strange sense of comfort in being cut off from the rest of the world with such cold totality. She glanced over at her cell phone still securely plugged into the electrical outlet to recharge its battery, her only link to civilization if she were to be snowed in.

"It could happen," Jeannie, her art rep, had warned with her usual sage type of wisdom. "You've got to be ready for anything up there in the mountains. We always keep the cabin stocked with nonperishables, candles, matches, and whatever you might need until you can be dug out, or the snow melts, whichever comes first. And either one might not be for weeks. So don't let that

November sunshine fool you, honey; you could get a blizzard at the drop of a hat."

Claire dropped her black felt walking hat onto the old maple table by the window and sighed deeply. Hopefully this change in weather wouldn't put a damper on her daily walks. Her hike through the woods seemed the only part of her day that she actually looked forward to, and she wasn't about to give it up to bad weather.

She looked again at her cell phone, this time even picking it up and fingering the small buttons. It wasn't too late to change her mind about all this. Maybe it was too extreme, or just plumb crazy, as her father had said from his home down in sunny Palm Springs. She quickly dialed Jeannie's number then waited impatiently for the assistant to put her on the line.

"Oh, Jeannie, I'm glad I caught you," she said finally, trying to disguise the tight feeling of unease that had crept inside her chest.

"Claire!" exclaimed Jeannie. "How's it going? Produced any masterpieces yet? I saw Henri just yesterday and promised him you'd have something very special for him in time for his holiday exhibition."

Claire groaned. "Don't make promises you can't keep."

"Oh, come on, kiddo. You've got to break free from this little slump of yours."

"*Little* slump?" Claire sighed deeply. "And, please, don't start another pep talk—"

"It's not a pep talk. It's just the facts. You know that I, of all people, hate to appear insensitive to the delicate nature of a talented *arteest*, but it's been over a year. You've got to move on, honey. Remember, *you* weren't the one

−6−

who died in that accident. You've got to keep living, kiddo. What would Scott think if he knew you'd quit your art like this. Or Jeremy for that matter—"

"Oh, stop, Jeannie!" The tightness in her chest exploded into hot, red sparks, and her pulse began to pound against her temples. "I don't even know why I listen to you!"

"Okay, okay." The voice on the other end instantly became calm and soothing. "I'm sorry, Claire, I really don't want to push you too hard. It's a good sign that you're actually getting angry with me—a healthy emotion, as my shrink would say. Now, listen to me. I want you to walk over to your easel right now—it is set up, isn't it?"

"Sure," lied Claire as she stared at her still unpacked art supplies lying heaped against the wall by the door, right where she had dropped them several days before.

"Okay, now go over and pick up a tube of paint—*any* color." Jeannie paused as if allowing time for Claire to follow her simple directions, although Claire did not. "Okay, now," continued Jeannie as if speaking to a small child, "just squirt a little paint onto your palette. . . . Now then, pick up a brush—*any* brush—and just start wiping that paint around on the canvas. Don't even bother trying to make it look like anything, Claire. Just start brushing it on—just swish-swish, free as the breeze. . . . You can even pretend that you're painting the side of a barn if you like, as long as you keep moving that brush. Like the Nike ad says, *just do it!* Okay, honey?"

Completely ignoring Jeannie's directions, Claire stared blankly out the front window, watching as white flakes floated down, filtering through pine trees, barely distinguishable against the sky. "It's snowing here," she said without emotion.

"Great. Perfect reflective light for painting. Now, you've got plenty of firewood and lots of provisions. Even if the electricity should go out you'll be absolutely fine; just remember to bundle up and keep that woodstove stoked up during the night."

Claire tried to remember why she'd called Jeannie in the first place. Certainly not for this. "Thanks, Jeannie," she said flatly. "I'll get right to work."

"Good girl." Jeannie paused. "And someday you'll thank me for this."

Claire sighed. "I sure hope so." She hung up and walked over to her art supplies, trying to remember exactly what it was that Jeannie had told her to do. It wasn't that Claire wanted to be difficult—and she knew that Jeannie *believed* she had her best interest at heart—it was just that Claire couldn't help it. But she would give it a try.

Mechanically, she released the bands from her easel, unfolded its spindly legs, then set it at an angle by the south window. Then she set up a small card table and slowly unpacked her art supplies, handling each single item as if she'd never seen such a thing before. She carefully arranged all her materials, lining up the brushes by width and size, fanning the tubes of acrylic paint into a perfect color wheel. She hadn't brought her oils with her. Perhaps it was laziness, or maybe she just wasn't ready to face that smell again. She stacked the clean palettes and folded her rags and set her water containers in a neat row, until the card table looked like an ad for an art supply store. With everything meticulously arranged, she stepped back and surveyed her work, nodding her head in grim satisfaction.

"Very nice, Claire," she said in a sarcastic tone. Never had she been so meticulous about her supplies. Usually caught up in the flurry of the creative process, she had been one to work like a chaotic whirlwind, surrounded by an incredible mess of squinched-up paint tubes, smelly rags, and dirty brushes soaking in grimy jars of mud-colored linseed oil. She remembered how Scott would step cautiously into her studio with a look of mock horror on his face.

"Oh, no, it looks like Hurricane Claire has struck again," he would tease. But then he would peer over her shoulder and praise—no, almost worship—her work. Never a critic, Scott had always believed her infallible as an artist and as a human. As a housekeeper, well now, that was another story.

Determined to obey her rep's directives, Claire opened a fresh tube of paint. Cobalt blue. She squeezed a generous amount onto her clean white palette. It was a harsh, cold, sterile shade of blue, and she knew nothing in nature that was exactly that color—other than her heart perhaps. Then randomly she selected a brush, "any brush," as Jeannie had instructed. And like a machine, she began to work the fresh paint back and forth across the clean palette. Swish-swish, swish-swish. Perfect consistency. Then she lifted the filled and ready brush, holding it just inches from the clean white canvas. And there her hand stopped as if her elbow joint had been flash frozen. She took a deep steadying breath and even closed her eyes, willing herself to move her hand forward, to make just one brush stroke.

"Do like Jeannie said," she told herself through clenched teeth. "Just pretend you're painting the side of a barn!" But her fingers locked themselves like a vise around the wooden brush handle, and the frozen arm refused to move. How long she stood there with her arm poised in midair she did not know, but finally she realized that the little cabin had grown dark and cold inside, and long, dusky shadows now stretched over the thin blanket of snow that had covered the ground outside. After cleaning the brush, she went to rescue the few small embers still glowing in the woodstove, throwing on some thin sticks of kindling and blowing fiercely until a tiny flame began to flicker at last. She warmed her hands over the tiny fire, then quickly added more logs, filling the stove and closing the door with a loud empty clang.

Without eating, she went to bed, pulling the thick eiderdown comforter up to her nose. And once again she dreamed of them. They were walking just ahead of her, close enough that she could recognize their straight backs and nicely squared shoulders; both had curly brown hair, the color of burnt sienna. And, although the boy's head didn't even reach the man's shoulder, they both walked with that same loose-jointed gait that told you they were related. Father and son. But as close as they seemed to her, they were always just out of reach—out of earshot. And no matter how hard she ran after them, screaming and yelling their names, they never turned to see her, they did not heed her voice. Only this dream was slightly altered from her usual one; in this dream they weren't walking on the beach, they were walking through the freshly fallen snow.

2

Claire awoke while it was still dark and wondered where she was, then realized by the chill in the air that this was the cabin. Too quiet and still and dark to be her loft apartment in the city. And far too cold. Across the room, she saw the small red embers, burned down low again, staring back at her like animal eyes. Hungry eyes. The fire craved more wood. She crawled out of bed, her bare feet cringing at the touch of the cold wood floor. Dragging the comforter along with her like a robe, she stuffed more wood into the woodstove, closing the door with a clank. Then she pulled the one easy chair over to the east window and, wrapping the comforter all around her, pulled her knees up to her chin and waited for morning to come.

At last she saw a sliver of golden light cutting through the dark silhouettes of evergreen trees. More snow had fallen during the night. It now looked to be several inches deep but not enough to prevent her from taking her daily trek to the little footbridge and back again. It was the one actual pleasure in her day. But she held it out for herself like a reward, her proverbial carrot for getting through what needed to be done.

It was upon arriving at the cabin that she'd made her detailed list of daily chores (things that Jeannie had told her must be done in order to survive). And then Claire had created a rigid schedule that, after only a week, she'd managed to stick to almost religiously. First she showered (whether she wanted to or not), then brewed a pot of strong coffee while she started herself some breakfast, usually oatmeal, canned fruit, and a piece of toast. These she forced down, mostly, reminding herself how the doctor had warned that to lose any more weight would seriously threaten her health. Afterwards, she would meticulously wash the dishes in the old soapstone sink, then carefully clean the small one-room cabin, plus bathroom, taking more time than she'd ever spent in her large rambling home before the accident, before she'd moved to her loft apartment.

When everything was spotless, she would go outside and restock the firewood box beside the front door as well as refill the copper washtub next to the woodstove. After this she split a small pile of kindling that went into the big wicker basket right next to the copper washtub—nice and neat. Finally she would carefully check her supplies to see if she needed to make the twenty-minute drive to the closest store for bread or eggs or fresh produce. And since she had made that trip just yesterday, the cupboards were nicely stocked. But today, thanks to the snow, she had two more tasks to add to her list. She picked up the old broom and neatly swept the powdery snow that had blown across the wide front porch. Then she found a snow shovel and shoveled through what couldn't have been more than four inches of light snow to create a little path that connected the small cabin to the nearby garage and attached woodshed.

Going back inside, she shook out the heavy suede working gloves that she'd located in the shed, placing them close to the fire to warm and to dry. She glanced at her watch and sighed. Just barely noon—she was getting too good at this. And so far she had not allowed herself to take her walk before two o'clock, on a pretense that she was "working" until then. Although she wasn't a bit hungry, she fixed herself a lunch of sliced apple and cheese and crackers, arranging them prettily on an old-fashioned plate of blue and white. This she set on the small maple table and slowly consumed, eating each bite slowly, yet barely tasting it. After brewing a small pot of green tea, she settled into the easy chair and opened a book on "igniting the creative spirit." She would attempt to read the first chapter, again, until two o'clock.

All morning long she had managed to ignore the card table with her neatly arrayed art supplies as well as the waiting canvas still standing at attention by the window. And she sat with her back to these instruments now, distracting herself with the black-and-white pages before her. Yet the words and letters danced off the smooth paper, never reaching the interior of her mind as she absently turned the pages. The familiar tightness in her chest was returning, and she glanced once again at her watch. Only one-thirty.

Gritting her teeth, Claire closed the book and stared out the window at the tall pine trees, their long needles clinging like slender fingers to fresh clumps of snow just starting to soften and melt in the sun. She *must* adhere to her schedule, she warned herself. Otherwise her little world would quickly fall apart and go spinning out of control. She closed her eyes and tried to pray, but as usual the words would not form themselves, would not come to her, not even in thoughts. Her heart recoiled within her, blank and empty—numb, except for that usual burning ache that never seemed to lessen, never seemed to leave her at all. And if, in fact, the pain were to leave, what would she be left with?

At exactly one-fifty-six she slowly rose from her chair and began to prepare for her walk. She laced up her sturdy leather hiking boots, wound a soft charcoal-colored scarf around her neck, buttoned up her heavy woolen coat, and placed her black felt hat on her head. Standing before a foggy antique mirror by the door, she stuffed her shoulder-length blond hair up inside the hat, then pulled the narrow brim down lower, clear to her eyebrows.

In the mirror her small pointed face looked ghostly pale surrounded by the severity of the black hat, and her eyes peered out from beneath the brim like two gray pools of sadness. But her ghostlike appearance hardly mattered since she never met anyone on her solitary walks. And, although she knew there were other cabins somewhere in this vicinity, she had yet to see a single person since her arrival, other than someone driving a dark red Suburban down the road too fast a couple of times, and of course, the old woman who ran the store at Saddle Springs. Claire slowly pulled on her knit gloves and looked at the clock over the kitchen stove. Ah, exactly two. Finally, she could set out on her walk.

She followed the same path every day, the only path she knew. It had been easy to recognize the trail before the first snow had fallen, since the packed-down dirt clearly marked the way through the woods. But now all was white. Fortunately, she'd memorized the way by now. She knew exactly how the narrow trail meandered through the pine forest, curving to the left then taking a sharp right turn at the big dead tree. The first time she had seen this huge, fallen juniper tree, she had actually wept. Seeing it laying there so helplessly, like old bleached bones with each branch still intact, had touched some hidden nerve within her. Obviously it had been cut down, for the old gray stump was sawn smoothly through, revealing faded rings from forgone years. But why had it been so mercilessly toppled like that? It had once been tall and majestic, one of the largest junipers in the forest. Why had it been left behind—not even used for timber? The sad waste of it all had overwhelmed her that first day, and she had stood there and mourned for the better part of an hour.

But with each subsequent day and walk, she'd grown accustomed to the fallen tree and now actually looked forward to seeing it, like an old friend. Its narrow top pointed like a twisty old finger directing her down the path where the woods would thin a bit and the trail would grow straighter. This thinning, she decided, was the result of an earlier forest fire, for she had spotted some large blackened stumps in the clearing, hunkered close to the ground like dark gnomes keeping their secrets close to their chests. And all around these hunchbacked darkened creatures grew smaller trees, healthy and supple and green, planted by nature to replace what had been so cruelly lost.

But today, as she walked along the path, everything looked altered and changed, draped in its fresh blanket of snow. Clean and white, pristine. Almost invigorating. But invigorating was an emotion she could only imagine and barely remember. Still, while walking along the forested area, she couldn't help but look around her in wonder.

Snow remained a novelty to one who had grown up in Southern California and only skied a few times in her life. Against the fresh blue sky, tall ponderosa pines stood like sentries, holding their rounded snowballs like artillery in their long, sparkling green needles. And fallen logs, previously dark and moldering, were now respectfully shrouded in clean white sheets, as if to rest in peace. She noticed sets of squirrel and rabbit tracks and some bigger tracks, maybe raccoon, crisscrossing each other here and there, and also the sharp two-toed spike tracks of dear. The pine forest wearing its first cloak of snow had become a new place. Strange and coldly beautiful.

She came to the old dead tree, just before the burn area, and actually gasped at its transformed beauty. Each twisted bare branch and gnarled twig, now dusted in a thin veneer of white powder and illuminated by the afternoon sun, glistened like polished silver and were a soft contrast against the brilliant blue backdrop of sky. The phrase "breathtakingly beautiful" had always sounded phony to her, but that is exactly how she would describe this scene. Before the accident she would have raced back to the cabin for her camera and then used a whole roll of film trying to catch every single angle and shadow and light just right. Then she'd have waited impatiently for the photos to be developed, imagining the final image in oils on a wide canvas. But now she simply stood and stared, almost afraid to breathe. Such beauty was terrifying to her now. She took a deep breath and continued to walk, leaving the fallen tree behind her, its image still burning itself into her brain, making it nearly impossible to see the trail ahead. Finally, after several minutes of walking, she regained her focus and began to look around again.

The clearing, void of tall tree shadows, grew so bright that she longed for her dark glasses, and for the first time she understood how it was that a person could actually become snow-blind. Even though her eyes were adjusting to the stunning brightness, she was still forced to keep them focused downward, mostly to the trail before her. And that's when she began to notice another type of tracks—in fact, two sets. *Human tracks.*

Claire frowned. Up until now she had imagined that this entire section of woods belonged to her, and to her alone. She thought of this as *her woods*. And she didn't want to share *her woods* with anyone who was walking on two legs. The tracks headed in the same direction she normally walked, the way she was walking right now. She knew she could choose to turn around and head straight back to her cabin. But as a result her walk would be cut short. Her only other option was to continue along her regular path and risk the chance of running into these two interlopers. Because surely they, like her, would eventually turn back and return to wherever it was they had come from—these people who were trespassing in *her* woods.

Oh, she knew this was all ridiculous. After all, the trail was part of the National Forest, put there for anyone and everyone to use and to enjoy. And she also knew that other cabins, spotted here and there, likely had inhabitants who relished the pleasures of a hike in the woods just as much as she, but up until now—with the help of the snow—she'd never seen any signs and had simply preferred to imagine that her little borrowed cabin was the only one within miles. It was that sort of isolation that had compelled her to come here; she had longed for that deep sort of loneliness—both within and without. Of course, Jeannie had mentioned there were others around, but she'd also said the majority of cabins sat vacant during most of the winter months. Too hard to get in and out of, too difficult to cross over the mountain pass once the snows came.

Claire kept walking, ignoring the human tracks and hoping she wouldn't come face-to-face with their owners and spoil her sense of isolation altogether. Hopefully this was a one-time thing, tourists who had stopped their car along the road to take a walk and enjoy the snow before continuing on their merry way. To her relief she walked all the way to the footbridge (her turn-back point) without seeing a living creature other than three brown does and a good-sized buck with a nice set of antlers. She turned back in triumph, pleased that she had *not* run into the owners of the human tracks as she walked back to the cabin. All in all, her leisurely paced walk usually took just less than two hours. Of course, if she walked faster she could probably cut that time in half, but then, why would she want to do that?

Back at the cabin she managed to distract herself from seeing her easel again, although she could feel its stiff presence, still standing guard at the window and perhaps even mocking her now. She was able to avoid it completely until it was nearly dark outside. And that didn't take long, for the darkness of imposing winter came more quickly with each passing day. Ignoring the electric lights, she lit a kerosene lamp and watched as its golden glow filled the room with a soft-edged, murky sort of light. She liked how the lamp created deep shadows, illuminating the wood surfaces with richness and warmth. And that's when her easel and art supplies faded into the shadows, into oblivion, finally allowing her to pretend they didn't exist at all.

She then began her evening routine. Not all that much different than the morning one. But after the last dinner dish was washed and dried and set into the old pine cupboard next to the sink, that familiar tightness began to build in her chest again. With each day (and it was always worse at night) it felt as if the burning, aching sensation was growing larger and larger, taking up even more space inside her. Instead of diminishing over time, it only seemed to increase. She had hoped that a drastic change like living alone in the woods might somehow change something—break something. But, if anything, it only seemed to amplify and magnify her pain and loneliness. And she knew she wasn't big enough to contain it all. In fact, she felt certain that in time she would simply burst open from it. And so, once again, she tried to pray.

Pressing her lips tightly together she closed her eyes and willed a prayer to form itself within her. *Please, God!* Only two little words, but it was a start and all she could muster. And as small and insignificant as it seemed, she felt surely it must be progress. As a result she relaxed a little, trying to remember the time in her life when she had known how to pray—a time when it had been as simple as breathing. Sometimes she had spoken the words out loud, but usually she just whispered them in the privacy of her own heart. Either way, she'd always been certain that God had listened. Up until the accident, that is. That's when the painful silence had begun. *Please, God!* her heart cried out again. *Please, please, help me.*

The next day, after a slightly better night's rest than usual, Claire finished her morning routine earlier than normal and decided to break her own rules by starting her walk *before* two o'clock. Another couple inches of snow had fallen during the night, almost but not completely erasing her steps from yesterday's walk. The fresh snow made it slightly more difficult to walk, but the effort was well worthwhile. The forest was stunningly beautiful, somewhat heartening, and nearly invigorating. *Nearly.* But once again, shortly after she reached the dead tree that pointed toward the clearing, she noticed the two sets of human tracks. Fresh tracks that had been made that day.

She stood for a long moment before deciding to simply ignore them and continue. But after only a few steps, she paused and examined the tracks more closely. She placed her foot next to the one imprint and noticed that it was quite a bit larger than her own boot—probably that of a man. Then she placed her foot beside the other imprint to find that these prints were smaller than hers. Obviously, a child's. So a man and a child had walked along this path today—and perhaps yesterday too. She sighed and continued on her way. She must simply forget that someone else had recently walked here—convince herself she was really alone in *her woods*. She would not consider the man and child hiking along somewhere ahead of her. But she couldn't help herself. Unwillingly, she began to envision the two walkers on the path before her. And it was an unwelcome image—that of father and son, laughing and talking as they walked along together. Alive and well, and enjoying life! It was like a sharp slap in the face, and it felt totally unfair—unjust even.

Reaching the clearing, she noticed how the two sets of tracks had left the main trail, diverting to the right. She followed the tracks with her eyes, curious as to where they might be going. And that's when she saw them. Like bas-relief images in white plaster, pressed into the snow were two distinct snow angels, their wings now glistening in the afternoon sun. She stood still, staring in wonder at the simple beauty of the snow art. It was the warm trickle of tears falling down her cold cheeks that reminded her it was time to move on, to force her eyes from this sight and forge ahead. She tried not to notice where the two sets of tracks came back onto the main trail again and continued before her.

But, as she walked along, her eyes focusing on the stumps and small trees, her original image of the strangers hiking on the trail up ahead of her altered—be it ever so slightly. Suddenly she envisioned the pair—father and son—striding along with a similar loose, long-legged gait. She imagined their curly, dark-brown heads the color of burnt sienna bobbing along, their straight backs and squared shoulders moving steadily forward. The painful familiarity made her swallow hard in disbelief. Then she blinked back fresh tears as her heart began to pound furiously. And suddenly she began to walk faster—much faster—until she was running breathlessly toward the bridge.

3

When Claire finally reached the footbridge, the tracks just kept going. She could see them curving off to the right, heading into the trees up ahead. Going where? She clung to the snow-covered wooden railing and gasped to catch her breath.

"Claire, you're crazy," she said out loud. She stared at the footprints continuing beyond the footbridge and seriously considered following them. But to where? And that's when she noticed that a thick band of clouds had rolled in, beginning to blot out the sunlight. These clouds were quickly filling the sky and were probably full of snow. But how could she not keep following the mysterious footprints? What if? She walked a short distance before she noticed that snowflakes were already tumbling from the sky. Not timid flakes, but large, heavy ones.

Shielding her eyes from the spinning flakes, she looked ahead but saw no sign of any living thing. She could barely discern the trail now washed in a swirling blur of white. These recently made tracks would soon be obscured by the rapidly falling snow—and yet . . . glancing over her shoulder, she looked at the trail behind her, only to see that it too was fading fast. Her heart pounded in her temples, echoing loudly in her ears. Whether it was exertion or fear, she wasn't sure. Perhaps both. She took a few more steps forward, knowing full well that she was making a foolhardy decision—or perhaps she was just slightly crazed—then she froze in her steps. Just whom was she following, *really?* She looked up to the moving mass of white above her and tried, once again, to pray. Raising both gloved fists into the air, she raged at God for her losses. Then, several minutes later, humbled by her own audacity, she meekly pleaded for his help. But this time her prayer was more than just a few words. Partially unintelligible perhaps, but it was an honest cry from the heart.

Finally she turned around and trudged back across the bridge and down what she hoped was the trail. The falling flakes abated slightly, and she was barely able to retrace the three sets of footprints, but by the time she reached the place in the clearing where the snow angels had been, she was disappointed to see that they had been nearly obliterated by the new snow. Taking advantage of this brief lull in the storm, and before she lost her trail completely, she jogged all the way back to the cabin.

Warm from her exertion, Claire paused on the cabin's covered porch to catch her breath as she peered out on the falling snow. It was coming down fast again, and the wind had picked up and was now swirling the flakes into moving walls that obscured all vision beyond twenty feet. As she shook off her snow-coated jacket and hat and gloves, she realized with chilling clarity how close she'd actually come to being out there in what appeared to be turning into something of a blizzard. "Thank you, God." She spoke the words aloud, almost startled at the sound of her own voice against the backdrop of the snow-muffled wind.

She stoked the fire and glanced up at the clock. It wasn't even two yet. She still had several hours to fill before the day would mercifully come to an end. Walking over to the window, Claire stared out onto the drape of whiteness that enclosed her. She could feel the canvas right next to her, still situated on its easel. It felt as if it were pulling her, tugging her toward it like a magnet. Could she?

Claire went over to the card table and looked at yesterday's pallet still stained with the stark unforgiving shade of cobalt blue. After setting it aside, she picked up a fresh white pallet, then looked blankly at the rainbow circle of paint tubes arranged so neatly on the card table. But it was as if the colors frightened or maybe just intimidated her, and finally, as if in surrender, she picked up a tube of titanium white. She held the tube in her hand, gently squeezing it, feeling it give beneath her fingers. Then she opened the cap and bravely pushed a small mound of paint onto the pallet. She stared at the stark white paint—barely distinguishable from the white pallet—then glanced up.

Peering out the window again, Claire studied the swirling, whirling whiteness before her. But it wasn't really pure white, she observed. She squinted her eyes as if to separate the tiniest traces of color hidden within its whiteness. No, it had a faint bit of green in it. Or maybe it was blue. And just a smidgen of black, to gray it ever so slightly in places. Taking up her pallet knife, she began to spread the white paint, adding just the faintest touches of green, blue, black . . . as needed. And like a woman possessed, she began to smear paint across the canvas, working faster and faster until the entire surface was covered. Washed in a sea of white.

Feeling weak and almost breathless from the effort, she finally stepped back and studied her artistic accomplishment. She stared at the whitened canvas for a long time and finally began to laugh, but it wasn't a mirthful laugh. Instead it was filled with self-doubt and deprecation. "Claire, you have totally lost it now." She threw down her pallet knife and wiped her hands on a damp rag, then collapsed on her bed in hopeless tears.

Several hours later, she awoke to a darkened cabin and the sound of the howling wind. But as she rose to check on the nearly dead fire, she thought she heard another sound as well. A quiet moaning sound—or perhaps it was simply the wind crying out of pure loneliness. Or maybe . . . maybe she was simply losing her mind altogether. She stood silently before the door, straining her ears to listen. And once again, she felt certain she was hearing another sound, something other than the wind.

She opened the door to a blast of cold and snow, and there huddled on her porch, just a few feet from the door, was some sort of animal. She started to back up and close the door as she remembered how Lucy McCullough, the owner of the small store, had recently told her about a rabid raccoon that had turned vicious on a family that had been "foolish enough to feed the durned thing." But this looked bigger than a raccoon. The animal slowly lifted its head, and despite its coating of snow, Claire could tell it was of a canine nature. But even so, she wasn't sure if it was wolf or dog—although she felt fairly certain there were no wolves in these parts. The animal moaned again, appearing to be in pain.

"Are you hurt?" she asked softly.

The animal struggled to its feet; she was certain it was a dog—some sort of shepherd mix. Still, she wasn't sure what to do. What if it was vicious or rabid? It walked slowly toward her, and when it got closer to the light coming from inside the cabin, she could tell by its eyes that it wasn't going to hurt her. She wasn't even sure how she knew this, but somehow she just did.

"Do you want to come in?" She held the door open wide, but the nearly frozen dog just stood there in front of the door, as if it were afraid to actually step inside.

"I won't hurt you," she promised, kneeling by the shivering dog. She carefully reached out her hand, keeping her fingers tucked into her palm the way Scott had once shown her long, long ago. The dog looked at her with soulful brown eyes, and she gently stroked his head. "Come on in, fella," she urged. "Come warm yourself by my fire."

She coaxed him into the cabin and shut the door against the storm. "You wait here while I get a towel to dry you with." She quickly wiped the snow off her bare feet and went to retrieve a couple of towels. Then, speaking in a calm voice, she led the dog over to the fire where she gently toweled him dry with one towel and, making a bed of the other, helped him to lie down. He looked up with appreciative eyes.

"What in the world are you doing out on your own on a night like this?" she asked as she looked through her cupboards for what might possibly be an appropriate meal for a half frozen dog. Finally deciding on a can of stew that she figured they both could share since she hadn't eaten dinner, she searched out a couple of earthenware bowls to use for the dog's water and food. She warmed the stew just slightly before generously filling his bowl.

The dog's tail began to thump against the floor as she situated the filled bowls before him. Then he stood somewhat unsteadily and began to lap, first from the water and then from the stew, which he quickly eliminated, licking the bowl clean as if to say thank you. Picking up the empty bowl, she noticed how he gingerly held his front left leg just slightly off the floor, as if it was hurting him. When he lay down again, she knelt to check it. She couldn't find any open cuts or wounds but noticed that he seemed to flinch when she touched what appeared to be a swollen joint.

"Did you hurt your leg, boy?"

His tail thumped against the floor, and he looked up with trusting eyes.

"Well, you'll just have to take it easy for now. Enjoy a warm night by the fire, and tomorrow I'll phone the store and see if anyone is missing you." She'd already noticed the dog wore no collar, but it was possible he'd slipped out of it. And surely old Lucy at the store would know if a dog had gone missing lately.

Claire set her bowl of stew on the table and sat down to eat, unable to take her eyes off this unexpected visitor. She'd never had a dog of her own. Her mother had always claimed they were too messy, and Scott, although he loved animals, suffered from allergies. And it wasn't that she'd ever really wanted a dog before, other than that short spell during childhood, somewhere between nine and ten.

She stoked the fire against the night and then refilled the dog's bowl with fresh water before she turned off the lights and made her way to bed. As she lay in bed, she remembered how utterly stricken she'd been earlier this same evening, and suddenly she realized how she no longer felt so completely helpless and hopeless. As odd as it was, this stray dog had provided a good distraction for her. Even now, seeing his silhouette by the firelight and hearing his even breathing brought a strange sense of comfort. But he's only a dog, she told herself, and someone is probably missing him right now.

Once again, she prayed. Only this time it came more naturally. Oh, it wasn't easy by any means, but she was at least able to form actual words and partial sentences in her mind, and somehow they made sense to her. She just hoped they made sense to God.

4

Claire awoke to something nudging her elbow. Startled from her deep and thankfully dreamless sleep, she looked over to see a pair of brown soulful eyes staring back at her. It took her a few seconds to remember last night's visitor, but it was obvious that the dog was still there, now peering at her in what seemed a fairly urgent manner.

"Poor thing," she muttered as she climbed from her bed. "I forgot all about you." Pulling on her robe, she glanced at the clock. "My goodness, it's after eight o'clock. I can't believe I slept that long." She reached down and patted the dog's head. "I'll bet you need to go out now, don't you?" She went to open the door, noticing once again how the dog painfully limped just to cross the room.

"There you go, boy." She waited as he slowly made his way through the threshold. "Now take it easy on that leg." She grabbed a few pieces of firewood then watched uneasily from the porch as the dog picked his way through what was now close to a foot of snow. Finally he relieved himself on a nearby tree. The weather seemed to be clearing up some with the promise of sunshine on the western horizon. The dog paused, sniffing the air, and Claire wondered if he might be thinking this break in the storm was a good time to return to his home. But it worried her to imagine him trying to make his way very far through the snow on that lame front leg. She knew he needed to give it a good rest.

But as if to show his good sense, the dog turned around and slowly limped back onto the porch. His tail wagged when he approached her, but once again he stopped at the door, as if waiting for another invitation to come inside.

"Come on in, boy. It's freezing out here, and I'll bet you'd like some breakfast." His tail wagged faster, and he followed her back inside the house, watching with patient eyes as she laid more sticks on the embers and blew to encourage the flames. "How about a real breakfast this morning?" she said, opening the refrigerator and pulling out an untouched carton of eggs. She scrambled up several and even grated some Swiss cheese on top while the bread toasted and the coffee perked. Then she dished up a good portion of eggs along with some torn-up pieces of toast into the same earthenware bowl she had used last night, even taking a moment to blow on the eggs to help them cool.

"There you go, boy." She set down the bowl. "Hope you don't mind eating people food." She dished up her own breakfast, but by the time she sat down at the table, the dog had already licked his bowl clean. "Guess you like my cooking."

Satisfied, the dog returned to his spot by the fire and carefully settled himself onto the makeshift towel bed, groaning just slightly as he licked the swollen joint that seemed to be troubling him.

After breakfast, Claire washed up the dishes to pass the time until nine when she could call Lucy at the store.

"Missing dog?" said the old woman. "You say you're missing a dog?"

"No," Claire corrected her. "I mean I have what must be a missing dog. He's at my house right now, but he's not mine."

"Oh. A stray, you mean?"

"He's a well-mannered dog. I'm guessing he ran away or got lost."

"Any ID?"

"No, he doesn't even have a collar."

"Well, he's probably a stray then."

"But he's an awfully nice dog, and he doesn't look malnourished, although he's got an injured leg. Have you heard of anyone who's missing a dog?"

"Well, let's see. Arlen Crandall lost his tabby cat 'bout a month back. But then that cat was as old as Methuselah, probably older than old Arlen himself."

"Any dogs missing?"

"Not that I've heard of. When'd you find him?"

"Just last night. He showed up at my door during the snowstorm."

"Lucky for him you took him in. It was pretty nasty last night—winds were up to forty miles an hour."

"Yeah, I'm glad I heard him over the wind."

"You say he's got a hurt leg?"

"Yes. He's limping, but I don't see an open wound or any sign of infection. Still, the joint is pretty swollen. I wonder if I should try to get him to a vet."

"Land sakes, no," said Lucy. Claire could hear her munching on something as she talked. "Don't waste good money on a vet for somebody else's dog. Besides, it's probably just a sprain, and ain't nothing no vet can do for a sprain anyway."

"I suppose. . . . Well, if anyone mentions a missing dog—he's some kind of shepherd or collie mix, I think—will you have them call me?" Claire repeated her cell phone number twice to make sure Lucy got it right, then hung up.

"Looks like you'll be hanging out with me for the time being," she informed the dog as she began working her morning schedule. But he seemed content to watch her from his post by the fire.

Once again, she completed her tasks more quickly than usual, and it was only eleven when she decided she'd break her daily routine for the second time. "No reason not to take a walk early today," she said as she glanced outside to see the sunlight breaking through. "Who knows, it could be snowing by two." She reached for her coat, then remembering, she glanced over at her disabled canine houseguest. "Oh." She frowned. "I'll bet you're not up for a walk, now, are you?" His tail thumped, but he didn't move from the warmth of his spot by the fire.

"No, of course not." She rehung her coat. "I forgot about your bad leg." She sighed and looked around the small cabin until her eyes came to rest on the canvas from yesterday. She stood and stared at the back of it for several minutes. She'd purposely avoided it all morning, but now she hesitantly approached it. Perhaps she was ready to examine her work more closely now. Maybe she would understand what it was she'd been trying to accomplish yesterday. She stood in front of the painting, her arms folded across her chest, and just looked. For a long time, she stared into it, hoping to see something—anything at all. But all she saw was white—shades upon shades of white.

Finally, to give her eyes relief, she redirected her gaze out the window, studying the snow-covered pines glistening in the sunlight. A pleasant scene, like something you might see on a Christmas card, but nothing spectacular. Nothing worthy of actually painting into a landscape. But then again, what would it hurt to try? It wasn't like she was doing much of anything else anyway. And so, once again, she arranged her paints on the pallet, some white and a bit of green and black. And then, with the scene out the window to guide her, she began to paint, carefully layering snow-covered trees to her blanket of white. She worked for several hours, but when she finally stopped, she felt disappointed. It was as if she'd become snow-blinded by her own creation, and for all she could tell it was simply layer after layer of unfeeling white. She turned from her work in frustration. "I *cannot* do this!" she exclaimed, throwing down her pallet knife in disgust.

She'd almost forgotten about her visitor and was startled to hear his tail now thump-thump-thumping against the floor. "Oh!" She looked over to see him sitting by the door. "I'm sorry. I'll bet you need to go out again." She reached for her coat and let him out, then went to the shed to fetch another load of firewood as she waited for him. But as she carried the wood back to the house, she noticed the dog had wandered over and sat down right next to the garage door.

"What is it, boy?" she called, stacking the firewood by her front door. "Don't you want to come back inside now?"

The dog remained there as if waiting for something. She walked over to the garage and patted his head. "What's up, boy? You think there's something interesting in there? Something you need to see?" She lifted open the garage door and held out her hand. "See, boy, it's just my Jeep." The dog limped over to the Jeep and stood right by the door, wagging his tail like he wanted to get in and go somewhere. "You want to get in the Jeep?" she asked incredulously. He sat down right next to the door and waited.

She scratched her head. "Looks like you want to take a ride, boy. Maybe you think we'll find your owners. Well, hang on while I go get my keys. I guess it wouldn't hurt to go down to the store and see if anyone's been looking for you."

Still, as she hurried back to the house to get her keys, she wasn't entirely happy about the prospects of discovering this sweet dog's owners. But suppressing these troubling thoughts, she helped load the injured dog into the passenger's seat and started the engine. She slowly plowed her way through the long driveway until she finally reached the unplowed road. "I thought Jeannie said they maintained this road year 'round," she muttered, maneuvering the Jeep through the snow. "Good thing I've got four-wheel drive." She smiled to herself as she remembered a few years back when Scott had picked out their new Jeep Cherokee. She had teased him over the unlikelihood that they'd ever actually need an off-road vehicle for their urban lifestyle in the Bay Area. "You just never know," he'd said with a twinkle in his eye.

"You just never know," she repeated as she glanced over at her well-mannered canine passenger. "Well, it sure looks like you've been in a car before." She half expected him to start barking when they reached a particular crossroad, like perhaps he was going to direct her to his home. But he just sat quietly, happily gazing out the window as if he rode around with strangers all the time.

After about thirty minutes of slow going, they reached the store and Claire carefully unloaded the dog. He stayed right at her heels, following her up to the front door. It hadn't even occurred to her until then that she didn't have a leash for him. But then she wasn't used to dogs or what to expect, and besides, this one almost seemed like he was leading her instead of the other way around. "Okay, you wait here, boy," she instructed him. "I don't know if Lucy likes dogs in her store or not." Obediently, as though he understood, the dog sat down on the porch.

The little brass bell on the door jingled as Claire entered, and old Lucy looked up from behind the cash register where she was reading a newspaper. "Hello there," she called.

"Hi, Lucy. I thought I'd stop by to—"

"No one's been in here today to complain 'bout a lost dog," she said with a frown as she folded her paper. "Fact is, ain't no one been in here today doing much of anything."

"Oh." Claire looked around the small but well-stocked store. "Well, I guess I might as well pick up a few things while I'm here then."

Lucy looked up with what seemed somewhat skeptical interest. "You still thinking you're gonna winter here?"

Claire nodded. "I—uh—I think so. Well, at least until Christmas."

"And you sure you're stocked up?"

"I think so."

"*Think* so? Or *know* so?" Suddenly Lucy was rattling off a list of all kinds of things—everything from toilet paper to coffee to canned meat to candles. "Just in case the electricity goes out, you know. We lost power for near a week a few years back when a tree blew down and took out the power lines with it. Not only that but a body can run out of all sorts of things during a long stint of being snowed in up here. You newcomers just don't understand what it takes to survive in the mountains when three feet of snow can fall within twenty-four hours."

"But my friend told me that the roads get plowed here . . . eventually."

Lucy rolled her eyes and laughed. "The key word being *eventually*. And unless you have a snowmobile or are ready to trek all day and night on snowshoes, you could be stuck but good. And you might as well know right up front that I don't make deliveries."

"Well, maybe I should pick up some extra things then," said Claire. "As well as some dog food and dog things."

By the time Claire got out of the store, she'd spent more than a hundred dollars and wasn't sure if she was being wise or had just been duped by a sharp old business-woman. Whatever the case, she figured she or someone else would use the supplies . . . eventually. The dog was still waiting on the porch.

"Hey, boy," she said as she opened a box of chew bones and gave him one. "You're a good dog." He quickly munched down the treat then followed her to the Jeep, watching while she loaded her supplies into the back. She paused to pull the new red collar from the top of the last box and bent down to slip it around the dog's neck. "Just until we find your owners, and in case I need to leash you up—not that I expect to—you seem to stay pretty close as it is. And it doesn't look like you'll be ready for a walk any time soon." Then she hoisted him back into the passenger seat. "Don't you look handsome." She stroked his smooth head and rearranged his collar so his tufts of ebony and honey colored fur hung neatly over it, then went around to the driver's seat.

"No one's called about you yet," she told him as she drove away from the store. Then she smiled—actually smiled. "But that's okay with me."

It was just getting dusky when they reached the cabin, and she wondered where on earth the day had gone. More snow was beginning to fall as she carried her supplies inside. Then, remembering Lucy's strong words of warn-ing, she decided to get a few more loads of firewood stacked on the porch before dark and even took time to chop some more kindling. As she worked—quickly, before the light faded—the dog stayed with her, limping back and forth between the house and the woodshed.

"You're such a good companion," she said as she finally stacked the last piece of wood by the door and brushed off her hands. "And I'll bet you're hungry now." Claire paused to stomp the snow off her boots. "I know I am." The realization of her statement hit her as she shook off her hat. "It's true, I'm actually hungry!"

5

Snow fell silently and steadily throughout the night. By the time Claire got up the next morning, there appeared to be about eighteen inches of accumulation. She took the broom along with her when she let the dog out, sweeping away the feather light powder that had drifted onto the porch. Taking in a deep breath of cold mountain air, she held it for a long moment, experiencing the chill in her lungs, then slowly exhaled. Lovely. It really was lovely. She hadn't noticed how clean and fresh it had felt before. The morning sun was peeking beneath a layer of clouds now, shining like a golden beacon through the trees, illuminating everything in its path with a wide stream of heavenly light.

If only she could take a walk today. She glanced over to the dog limping back toward her, his tail wagging. His leg did seem slightly better, but not well enough for a walk.

And how could she leave her poor faithful companion all alone? What if he didn't understand? Or thought she had abandoned him? No, her daily walks would have to be kept on hold for a while longer.

"I wish you had a name, boy." She patted him on the head. "Well, I suppose you do have a name. I just don't know it." She thought for a minute. "Maybe I should just give you one." But what if she gave him a name and then his owners suddenly showed up to collect him. Perhaps it was better not to get too attached. Or to wait and see what happened first. She finished up with her outdoor chores, shoveling the paths, stacking more wood, and chopping more kindling.

"Maybe old Lucy was right," she said to the dog as she stomped the snow off her boots. "I suppose we could get snowed in here." She squinted up at the morning sun still filtering through the trees. "Although that doesn't seem very likely right now."

Back in the cabin, she wondered what she could do to pass the time. She stood and studied her snowy painting from the previous two days and finally just shook her head. "An exercise in futility," she muttered. Then she removed the canvas, leaned it against the wall, and replaced it with a blank one. Once again she stood for a long while, just staring out the window, gazing on the patterns of light and shadows that played through the trees. Could she possibly capture it? And what would it hurt to try?

She worked so long and hard that she completely forgot about lunch, and only when the outside shadows grew long and somber did she pause to turn away from her work and finally look up at the clock. "Good grief!" She noticed the dog now standing at her feet, looking up expectantly, as if he needed to go out again. "Whatever happened to the day?"

She set aside her brush and let him out, taking a moment to stretch her stiff arms and shoulders and shaking the cobwebs out of her head as she breathed in the fresh icy air. "Hey, it looks like you're walking better now, boy." She bent down and gave him a good scratch behind the ears. "Tell me, do you have a master somewhere? Someone who's looking for you and missing you just desperately?" She shook her head. "Well, if you were my dog, I'd have been combing the neighborhood for you. And the first place I'd have checked was Lucy's store." She stood up. "And if no one calls for you by tomorrow, well, we're giving you a name—and that's that."

After stoking up the faltering fire, she fixed dinner for them both, then busied herself with cleaning and straightening—afraid to allow herself to go back and review her day's work. She knew she would only be disappointed with a painting that held nothing more than snow and trees and, oh yes, light. And although the snow scene was better than a blank canvas, it certainly wasn't a landscape that Jeannie could interest Henri, or anyone else for that matter, in showing. But at least she was painting. That was something. For three days now she had actually worked— a real breakthrough. And it seemed no coincidence that this change had come only after she'd really broken down and prayed to God to help her. She hung a polished copper pot back on the rack and thought. Hadn't that been about the same time that the dog had come into her life too?

So that night when Claire went to bed, she remembered to thank God for sending help. Maybe it did come in the form of a dog, but it was help just the same, and she knew it. Now if only she could keep this dog.

The next morning she awoke to the sound of her cell phone ringing. Certain it must be Jeannie checking up on her, she eagerly jumped out of bed, ready to tell her (and honestly this time) that she'd actually made a little progress—that she'd been painting! But it was a man's voice on the phone, and one she didn't recognize.

"This is Rick Marks," said a gruff voice. "I hear you've got my dog."

She felt her heart plunge like a rock as she looked at the dog now wagging his tail at her feet. She could tell he was ready to be let out. "Did you lose a pet?" she asked weakly as she walked across the room to open the door for the dog.

"Yeah, he ran off."

"Really?" She thought about this. "Are you sure this is your dog? I mean, he doesn't really seem like the type to run off—"

He laughed, but not in a nice way. "Aw, that mutt's always running off."

She didn't like this man calling the dog a mutt. "Well, maybe you should describe him to me. Maybe we're not talking about the same dog."

But when Rick described the shepherd-collie mix right down to the patch of white beneath his chin, she knew they were talking about the same dog. "What's his name?" she asked in a quiet voice.

"Mike."

"Oh." She looked out the window to see the dog, rather, Mike, now making his way back onto her porch, his limp barely noticeable. "What happened to his leg?" she asked, not even sure why, perhaps only as a stall tactic.

"His leg?"

"Yes, he had a bad leg when he first showed up."

"Well, he was perfectly fine last time I saw him."

She sensed hesitation in his voice and felt a flicker of hope. "Does that mean you might not want him back?"

"Aw, he's my dog, lady. Of course, I still want him back."

"Right." She mechanically gave him directions to her house. "But that snow's pretty deep," she added. "And the roads haven't been plowed over here. Are you sure you can make it here okay?"

"It'd take a heck of lot more snow than this to keep me off the road."

Claire dressed quickly, then made sure that Mike got a good meal before his master arrived to take him away. After the dog finished licking the bowl clean, Claire knelt down on the floor and wrapped her arms around the soft fur of his neck. "You are such a good dog," she said. "I can't believe you're going to leave me now." She ran her hands down the silky coat on his back. "Thank you for coming to—to—" Her voice broke, and she buried her face in his neck and sobbed for several minutes. Finally she stopped, feeling his warm wet tongue now licking her face, as if to comfort her.

At the same time she heard the rumble of an engine pulling up her driveway. The dog's muscles tightened when the sound grew louder, and his ears peaked to attention. Then he gave a low growl and a couple of sharp barks. It was the first time she'd heard him bark. She peered out the window to see one of those ridiculously tall pickups with the huge oversized tires plowing up her driveway. It was painted a garish metallic blue and was trimmed with a row of lights that made it look like something from another planet. A heavyset man in a plaid flannel shirt climbed out and ambled up to her door, knocking loudly and causing the dog to bark again.

She stood by the door for a moment, unsure whether she actually wanted this man to come inside her house, much less to know that she was living out here all alone. Finally she decided to simply step outside with the dog.

"Hello," she said stiffly as she closed the door behind her.

He tipped his head slightly then grinned as he carefully took in her appearance. "Howdy, ma'am. I don't recall catching your name."

She forced a smile. No sense in being hostile. "My name's Claire."

"You're new 'round here."

She nodded. "Yes. Just visiting. It's my friend's cabin."

"Well, I still don't know how Mike found his way clear over here," said Rick, scratching his head as he looked at the dog. "It's time to go home, buddy. Go get in the truck now."

But the dog just sat there, as if rooted to the porch next to Claire's feet. She restrained herself from reaching down to pat his head and say, "good dog."

"I *said*, go get in the truck, Mike!" Rick spoke in a sharp tone and pointed to the pickup. The dog began to slowly walk toward the truck, his tail pointed straight down like a rod.

"He's better, but his leg's still hurting him some," said Claire, following the dog with her eyes. "He might need some help getting up there."

Rick made a snorting laugh. "Well, I guess I could give him a hand, just this once. There's no sense in pampering your animals too much." He easily hoisted the dog into the pickup bed that was partially filled with snow, then stepped back. Claire noticed there was no tailgate on the truck.

"Won't he slip out and hurt himself?"

Rick laughed again. "He's ridden like this his whole life." Then he noticed the collar and quickly slipped it off. "And he don't need no fancy collars neither." He handed it to her. "Sorry that he troubled you."

"He was no trouble." Just then Claire considered offering him money for the dog, wondering if that would be an insult or not. "Uh—you wouldn't be interested in selling Mike, would you?"

He laughed again. "Nah, my other dogs have been acting up since he's been gone. He may not be much, but he's a good ol' dog."

She nodded, fighting to hold back tears and telling herself she was a fool for caring so much in the first place. "Yeah, he is." Then she turned back to the house, unable to look at the dog again, afraid she would completely break down in front of this less than sensitive man.

She listened as the truck's loud engine started up again and waited until the sound became a dull rumble then faded away to nothing before she collapsed on her bed and sobbed uncontrollably. "Why, God?" she cried. "Why would you send this sweet dog to comfort me and then just snatch him away? Why?"

6

Claire was unable to paint a single stroke for the remainder of the day. Instead, she paced about the cabin like a caged animal, cleaning and straightening what already looked perfectly neat. Finally at two o'clock sharp she allowed herself to leave the confines of the cabin. The snow was well over a foot deep now—the deepest she'd walked in so far—and it made for hard work, not to mention slower. But she didn't care. Perhaps the effort would be so taxing that she might forget all about the dog, at least temporarily. She should've known better than to let her heart become so attached—and to a silly animal! She trudged steadily along, hardly lifting her eyes from the ground, just following the trail—step after step—until she finally reached the dead tree. There she stopped to catch her breath and look around. But instead of seeing the beauty she'd been so fascinated by before, everything looked dull and flat and starkly white to her. Uninteresting even. And now a lifeless layer of heavy cloud hung low overhead. It was the color of an old nickel and probably filled with more snow. But she didn't really care. Let it snow.

She turned to the right, as usual, and began moving toward the old footbridge, when she noticed those same two pairs of footprints as she'd seen before. Due to her recent distractions, first with the dog and then her painting, she'd almost forgotten about those sets of disturbing footprints. But now, here they were once again, and with fresh clarity, as if they'd just been made today. And while they weren't quite as distinct as before because, like her, the walkers had been forced to trudge along slowly cutting their way through the thick snow, they were clearly the same sets of footprints—one large, one small. She walked along, following them, unwilling to step right in their tracks; yet, it was much easier to walk where they had already stepped. Once again, she wondered, to whom did they belong? Who had been out here walking in all this snow today? Perhaps they'd passed by just moments ago, for the imprints appeared fresh.

Maybe it was because she was tired, or simply just sad, but it didn't take long before she began to imagine the two of them again. Father and son, strolling along—maybe they were hand in hand this time, the dad helping the boy through the deep snow, but still they'd be walking with that slow, distinctive gait. She tried to go faster now, hoping to spy them as she came around the bend in the trail up ahead, but when she turned the corner all she saw was snow and trees. And more snow and trees . . . nothing but snow and trees.

By the time she reached the bridge, the clouds had grown thicker and darker, and she knew she should turn back, but somehow she just couldn't. And as tired as she was, she continued, panting breathlessly as she trudged through the thick layer of snow, following doggedly without looking up. Finally, maybe thirty minutes later, she noticed fat snowflakes were falling quickly now, and, despite her desperation to find the mysterious walkers, she knew she must turn back. For the second time, she had embarked on a fool's errand, and one that could easily turn lethal if she didn't return to her senses.

She couldn't even be sure how she finally made it back to the cabin that late afternoon. But somehow she did. By the time she reached her driveway, her vision was almost completely obscured by the swirling snow and a bluish light that was fading fast. She went inside, stripped off her snow-coated, sweat-soaked clothing, and collapsed into bed without even eating dinner.

That night she dreamed she was caught out in the woods—in the midst of a howling blizzard and waist high snow. She was freezing cold, and as hard as she tried, she couldn't push her way through the deep snow. She felt trapped in quicksand and could feel herself being pulled down, down, down. And after a while she lost all strength to resist. She no longer cared. She entirely lost her will to fight. Better to give in, to just allow its cold forces to swallow her up. And then she would be no more. Feel no more. Escape.

But just as she yielded, resting her face in the cold, white snow, two angels appeared—one on either side. They were brilliantly white, even whiter than the snow! She couldn't see the features on their faces because they glowed so brightly—like burning kerosene lamps. Still she could feel them near her, and each one held securely to an arm as they guided her through the snowstorm. They even lifted her up as if she were lighter than a rag doll, her feet trailing helplessly through the snow. And then they carried her up higher, as if she were lighter than a feather, and the three of them flew like birds above the evergreen treetops, up over the falling snow and the layer of clouds. She wanted to ask the angels their names but was so awed by them she was unable to find her voice to speak. It was a delightful dream, really, and she was sorry to wake up. But flying through the snowstorm with the angels had made her cold, and when she awoke, she was shivering in the darkness.

She looked across the coal-black room to see the fire had gone completely out. And why not, when she hadn't even bothered to stoke it up after her wild and reckless walk? Now she paid for her mistake as her feet touched the icy floor and she struggled with freezing fingers to wad up old newspaper and stack the kindling. Her hands shook from the cold as she lit a match and held it to her little mound, blowing gently to help the fragile flame grow stronger.

Wrapped in a quilt, she huddled before the fire for more than an hour before she finally began to feel free of the icy grip that had laid hold of her. And by then, despite the hour, she was wide awake and unable to sleep, still fascinated by her captivating dream. Finally, she made a pot of strong coffee and went over to look at her two recently painted canvases, hopeful she might see something worthwhile in their content. She stared for a while then frowned. Nothing more than boring snowscapes—layers of white upon white upon white. Lifeless and blah. Not even good enough to be reproduced into Christmas wrapping paper!

How long she stood there, she couldn't remember, but suddenly like a flash of light in the midst of hopeless darkness, it hit her. She moved a couple of lamps nearer her easel, then picked up a fresh pallet and opened a tube of paint. Those paintings simply weren't finished yet.

She worked with a frenzy—a creative compulsion unlike any she'd ever known before—only pausing on occasion to stretch out her stiff arm and briefly sip on her long since cold coffee. Still working, she hardly noticed when the sun came up, although she appreciated the improved light, but she continued relentlessly on until it was nearly noon. Finally, her back and shoulders burned like fire and she was forced to stop, to step back and simply close her eyes.

Without even allowing herself the opportunity to pause and evaluate her work (for fear she would be sadly disheartened) she turned toward the kitchen area and opened a can of tomato soup, quickly heated it, then sat down at the table to eat in silence. She imagined how she must look, unwashed and unkempt, huddled there still wrapped in the worn quilt, eating her lukewarm soup with only the sound of the clock ticking and the clink of the spoon against the ceramic bowl.

"I'm a madwoman," she said aloud as she set the empty bowl into the sink with a loud thunk. Suddenly, she imagined her favorite artist—Vincent Van Gogh—and the way he had cut off his ear and done other strange things, and for the first time she thought perhaps she almost understood. Sighing loudly, she paced the floor, careful to keep from accidentally seeing her recent painting, still unwilling to look at her work. "And now I'm even starting to talk to myself," she mused.

Then in sheer exhaustion, she stoked her dwindling fire and allowed herself a short nap before she returned once again to her unsettling creation. She worked until dusk this time and, lamenting the loss of good light, turned the easel toward the wall (still afraid to really look) and fixed herself a bowl of undercooked oatmeal for dinner. She knew her eyes were too tired to keep painting anymore tonight, especially if she didn't want to sacrifice the quality of her work—assuming there was any quality. And so she simply sat in the easy chair and closed her burning eyes, wondering how in the world she would ever be able to survive this soul-wrenching loneliness. It was odd though, while she had definitely felt the pain of loss, she hadn't really noticed the loneliness so much before. In fact, her solitude had been somewhat welcome when she'd first come to the cabin. But somewhere along the line, something in these circumstances had changed. Maybe it was her.

Just then, she heard a scratching sound followed by a sharp bark.

"Mike!" she cried, leaping from her chair and dropping the quilt to the floor. Sure enough, when she flung open the door, there was the dog all covered with snow. She told him to come, and, as he gave himself a shake, she ran for the towel, happily drying him off by the fire.

"Oh, what on earth are you doing out in this horrible weather, you silly old dog?" Then she hugged him, and he wagged his tail. "I'll bet you're hungry." She quickly found his dishes and filled them with food and water. She set them before him, watching with pleasure as he hungrily devoured every bite. She knew she should contact Rick. But she didn't have his phone number. And besides, it was dark out, and she wasn't eager to see him standing on her doorstep tonight. It would have to wait until morning. In the meantime, she would simply enjoy this unexpected visit from her dear old friend.

Having Mike (or Michael as she had decided to call him) made it easier to go to bed that night. It was such a comfort to hear the dog's even breathing as he slept by the warmth of the fire. But before she drifted to sleep she prayed. First she thanked God for returning Michael to her, and then she asked that she might somehow keep him for good this time. She knew it was a long shot but figured she had nothing to lose.

The next morning she awoke early, refreshed by a good night's sleep. She couldn't actually remember if she'd dreamt of angels again or not, but she was heartened to see her friend Michael still sleeping peacefully by the fire. But his head popped up as soon as he heard her footsteps. Soon his tail was thumping against the planks of the wood floor, and she knew he was waiting to be let out. She watched him make his way down the porch and into the snow, his limp barely noticeable now. She knew she had to make some kind of an attempt to reach Rick today, but she was in no hurry. And once again she prayed that God would somehow allow her to keep Michael.

After breakfast, she went over to yesterday's canvas and hesitantly turned the easel around, allowing the morning light to wash across it. She felt her hand go to her mouth as she gasped in wonder. Had she really painted *that?* She moved closer and, narrowing her eyes, studied it carefully. Incredible! There amidst the trees and snowy background she'd painted a few days back were several—what would she call them—celestial beings? No, they were simply angels. And they were artfully tucked here and there, almost so that you wouldn't notice. Some angels were partially hidden behind trees, some translucently visible in the foreground. But each angel was painted in varying shades of white—in fact the entire picture was little more than shades of white upon white. If you squinted, it looked like little more than a snowstorm. But if you looked closely, the angels were clearly there. It was amazing, really. She closed her eyes and shook her head sharply, then looked again—almost thinking she'd imagined this whole thing or was dreaming again.

"Did I really paint that?" she said aloud, drawing the attention of Michael who walked over and looked up with canine curiosity. She turned to him. "What do you think, boy?"

His tail wagged as if to give approval, although Claire knew he was simply responding to her voice. And then she began to laugh. "Oh, man, Jeannie's going to think I've gone totally off the deep end." She went to put on the coffee. "First of all, I'm talking not just to myself but to a dog as well. And next off, I've started to not only believe in angels but to paint pictures of them too."

She took her coffee mug back over to the painting, ready to look again, to see if it was really as good as she'd first thought. Perhaps she wasn't really seeing things as they were—another symptom of insanity. But this time she liked the painting even more. Of course, this alone should have disturbed her since she didn't usually like her finished work at all. And despite the opinions and approval of others, she was always her worst critic. "Maybe I am losing it, Michael," she said, taking a sip of hot coffee. "But I really think God's sending me angels to help me through this—this thing." She reached down and patted his head. "And if I'm smart I'll keep this little bit of information to myself. But I honestly think you might be an angel too."

Still, and as much as she hated to, she knew she needed to make an attempt to reach Rick. Finally, she decided to just get it over with and dialed information, but was informed that his number was unlisted. She decided to call Lucy at the store and see if she might know something more.

"Yeah, Rick got your number from me the other day, but he didn't bother to leave me his number for you." Lucy cleared her throat. "He's not the friendliest guy around, if you didn't notice."

"Well, he picked up his dog the other day, but late last night he came back."

"Rick?" Old Lucy let out a hoot. "Why, he's a married man—still, I wouldn't put it past—"

"No, no. Not Rick. The *dog* came back."

"Oh, well, that's not so bad. But still, that's a nuisance now, isn't it? Rick ought to be fined for letting his animals run wild like that."

"I don't really mind. I mean I like the dog, a lot. I honestly wish Rick would let me buy the dog from him."

"Well, why don't you then?"

"I offered, but he didn't seem too interested."

Lucy made a noise that sounded like *harrumph*. "Well, from what I've heard, that man has more dogs than a body needs, and his own family hardly has food on the table. Fact is, he's run up his bill at the store again."

Claire sighed. "Well, if you see him, would you tell him I'm willing to pay good money for this dog?"

"*Good* money?" Lucy laughed. "You sure you want me saying it just like that? Don't you know he's bound to take advantage of you?"

"Well, say it however you think best. You're the businesswoman, Lucy."

"That's absolutely right, honey. You leave it all up to me and I'll have that man paying you to keep his dog."

"Oh, I don't want that—"

"Well, one way or another, you just trust me, and I think we can work this thing out just fine."

"Thanks, Lucy."

"By the way, how's your painting coming along these days?"

"Actually, I think I've made a real breakthrough."

"Well, good for you, honey. You keep it up now."

Claire hung up the phone feeling slightly more optimistic. She knew Lucy would be a better match against someone like Rick than herself, but she still wasn't too sure he'd be willing to part with his "good ol' dog" as he'd put it. Although, now that she thought about it, she'd given up awfully easily. She knew Lucy wouldn't give in like that.

Claire got out the other snowscape now, the second one she'd painted, the one with beams of sunlight filtering through the trees. With trembling hands, she set it on the easel and stepped back. But before she picked up a brush, she closed her eyes and breathed deeply, attempting to remember the vivid angel dream from the previous night. And then she prayed that God would guide her hands, and her heart, and she began.

It was after two o'clock by the time she paused. She felt Michael's nose pressing against the back of her calf, as if to gently get her attention. She sighed and stepped back, glancing down at the dog. "I'll bet you need to go out again." He wagged his tail. Noticing hunger pains, she grabbed an apple and a chunk of cheese; the latter she shared with Michael, then she got her coat and hat and headed out the door.

"I think you could use a little exercise today," she said, heading toward the road. "Not too much, mind you, but just enough to keep that leg getting stronger." They walked slowly down the trail; it was still slightly packed from yesterday's trek, although a fresh layer of snow softened her previous tracks. The sun was trying to break through a thin veneer of fog that hung suspended through the trees like a transparent fluffy quilt, resulting in a soft, gentle sort of light—almost heavenly. It would be the perfect backdrop for her next painting! She paused now and again, allowing Michael a chance to rest his leg as she tried to memorize the scene before her. Would she be able to capture that kind of mysterious light, that downy softness? She played with various ideas for technique while she walked, praying once again that God would continue to lead her along this intriguing artist's journey she seemed to be on.

She went as far as the dead tree, curious whether or not she'd see those two sets of tracks today. But spying no fresh tracks, she decided to turn back. "I think this is far enough for you, Michael." She felt a keen sense of disappointment as they walked back. She had so wanted to see those tracks again, for as much as they disturbed and frightened her, they also gave her a strange sense of hope. Oh, she knew they couldn't *really* be angels—at least not likely—because angels surely wouldn't go tramping through the woods in snow boots. And she knew it wasn't *really* Scott and Jeremy—despite her wild imaginings. For that was impossible and ridiculous, a little insane even. But something inside her, something she dared not consciously consider let alone acknowledge, still longed for a miracle.

7

Claire dreamed of Scott and Jeremy again. This time it was the old familiar beach scene with them just up ahead and her unable to catch up or make them aware of her presence. And once again she awoke with pounding heart and clenched fists—frustrated that she couldn't even catch a glimpse of their faces. She got out of bed and though it was still quite early and very dark, she turned on lights and threw fresh wood on the fire. Michael watched her curiously but didn't budge from his cozy bed by the hearth.

"It's okay, Michael," she said soothingly as she quietly closed the woodstove door. "You can't help that you've linked yourself up with a madwoman. Don't mind me. I think I'll just work on my painting a little." And so she returned to her easel and the third canvas she'd started during the last week. She was trying to capture the misty light from their walk the previous day. She knew it would be a perfect backdrop for more angels—if they would only come to her again. She'd hoped to have that dream, the one where they lifted her up to fly. But instead she'd been frustrated by the old one, and it was still haunting her now. Perhaps she could lose herself and forget about it in the process of painting.

It took Michael's nudge of reality to bring her back into the present. She paused long enough to let him out and fix them both a bit of breakfast. But then she went straight back to her work. This picture felt special somehow—as if it might actually capture the images of Scott and Jeremy. Of course, she knew the departed weren't actually real angels—she'd gone to Sunday school and church long enough to know that. Angels were heavenly beings, created by God, who went as messengers and helpers and whatnot . . . while humans, once in heaven, were supposedly given heavenly bodies (although how could one really know for sure until that day came?) and were supposed to be somehow *different* from angels. Now what exactly that difference was, or how it looked, was a complete mystery to her. And so, if she wanted to imagine her deceased husband and son as angels, well, who on earth was going to argue with her about it?

It wasn't until the late afternoon shadows came that she realized she had painted too long for them to take their daily walk. "I'm so sorry, Michael," she said, glancing at the clock and setting her brush down. "We could still go out for a bit and stretch our legs."

The snow was a dusky blue now, and when Claire looked to the eastern sky, she could see a nearly full moon shining through the trees, casting its pearly shadow through their black silhouettes. She stood in awed amazement, wondering once again if she could feasibly capture this beautiful work of creation. Would it be possible to reflect this kind of magical twilight in the medium of mere paints and canvas? And even if she could, would the angels work with it? And was she absolutely crazy to go on painting these snowscapes with angels anyway? Who would ever be interested in such things? It was highly possible that she had become compulsively obsessed with something that everyone else would just laugh at or dismiss as too sweet and overly sentimental.

She picked up the stick that Michael had just dropped at her feet and tossed it across the snow again. Not that her angels were childish or cherublike by any means. No, with her impressionist style they came across as more mysterious and strong and active—in motion somehow. At least that's how it seemed to her. But, she wondered as she impatiently waited for Michael to return with the stick again, what about what she'd painted today? Was it really what she thought it was? Was it all she hoped it would be? Who was she fooling anyway?

"Come on, boy!" she urged, heading back to the porch, stomping her boots as she opened the door.

She didn't allow herself to view the painting until she fixed them both a good dinner and cleaned up afterwards. After making herself a cup of strong tea, she set a floor lamp next to her easel and turned the easel so it faced the easy chair. Then she situated herself comfortably in the chair and looked up, unsure of what she expected to see. The painting looked different in the cabin's mellow golden lamplight—more alive and real somehow, as if the faces contained expressions she hadn't even painted there. She stared in silent wonder for a long while—until the tea in her cup grew as cold as the tears on her face. Then she slowly rose from the chair, turned off the light, and prepared for bed.

The next morning she didn't look at the previous day's painting. Promising herself to begin her twilight painting as soon as she finished her chores and took Michael for a short walk she set the haunting painting aside—in a dark corner where she could barely see it. Her reason for wanting to take an earlier walk was twofold (if the truth were to be known). Partly so she could be back in time to paint until evening when she might once again catch a glimpse of the moonlit scene, and partly in case she and Michael decided to walk further—to see where those footprints in the snow really went. She felt she owed it to herself—not to mention her sanity—to do so. But just as she was washing the last breakfast dish, the phone rang.

"I hear you got my dog over there again."

"Hello, Rick." She tried to make her voice sound cheerful and pleasant.

"Lucy's been telling me you want to buy him."

"That's right." Remembering Lucy's warning, she tried not to sound overly eager.

"Well, I told Lucy that I ain't too interested in selling him, but then she reminded me how my bill's just a little overdue—" He made a shushing sound. "I know, Lucy. Just give me a minute, would you?"

"Are you at the store right now?"

"Yeah, and Lucy's here acting like she's some kind of dog broker or something, like she's supposed to be handling all this for you."

"Well, I told her to go ahead and make you an offer."

"Like I said, I'm not real eager to sell Mike. He's a good—"

"Gimme that phone, Rick." It was Lucy's voice now. "Okay, Claire, if you want, I'll just handle this for you. You just give me the word, and I'll strike a deal that everyone can be happy with."

"Sure, Lucy. Do what you think is best. I just want to be certain I get to keep the dog, but I sure don't want him to cost a fortune either. Not that he's not worth it. Let's see, I'm willing to go a hundred dollars to start with."

"Nah, you're right, he's not worth much. I think thirty bucks is a right generous offer too."

"Thirty?" Claire frowned. "I just said—"

"Now, I myself wouldn't have given Rick a dollar for that old mutt."

"But, Lucy—"

"Well, Rick's standing here holding up five fingers in front of my nose and saying 'fifty.'"

"Fifty is fine!" Claire said with excitement. "I'll gladly pay—"

"Claire says she won't go over forty, Rick. How old's that dog anyhow?"

"Lucy!" yelled Claire. "I'll pay fifty!"

"Four years old, you say." Lucy made a tsk-tsk sound. "Why, ain't that about half a lifetime for a mutt?"

"Please, Lucy!" Claire looked down at Michael hopefully.

"Okay, Rick, Claire has agreed to forty-five. But that's her final offer."

"Lucy!"

"All right, honey. It's all settled. Forty-five it is. That'll just cover Rick's bill and that pack of cigarettes he's pocketing right now. The dog is yours—you can settle up with me later."

"Thanks, Lucy." Claire felt slightly weak. "But I'd be happy to give him fifty."

"You drive a hard bargain, honey, but Rick is holding at forty-five."

Claire's hand was shaking as she set down her cell phone. "That woman!" Then she turned to the dog. "Michael, you really belong to me now!"

The sun shone down brightly as they set out for their walk that morning. Its warmth made the snow soften and melt, sinking down into itself. This also made for easier walking and distinct footprints. But when they reached the tree, she found no new sets of footprints—only faded mushy ones from days before.

"Oh, well," she said as she turned around. "I have enough to be thankful for today." She patted Michael's head. "You belong to me now."

She spent the afternoon trying to recapture the mood and colors of the twilight evening and moon from the night before. It felt odd to be using such dark colors on the canvas this time—lots of blue and black. And she didn't really like it. Finally, late in the afternoon, she stopped, realizing that this was her chance to go see it again. She bundled up and then carried a kitchen chair out onto the porch, settling herself in to witness the spectacle unfold.

As she watched the shadows grow longer, the dusky blue of the snow, and finally the now full moon appear, it occurred to her that the colors here were quite similar to Van Gogh's *Starry Night*. She waited a while longer until a few stars appeared and thought perhaps that was what the scene was missing. Then, chilled from the cold, she and Michael went back inside where she fixed their dinner with golden stars still dancing in her head.

And then she painted. Late into the night, she worked, thinking (or just hoping) that she was finally getting it. Whatever *it* was. But it was three in the morning by the time she quit, falling exhausted into her bed with her clothes still on.

The phone awakened her, and groggily she answered, afraid it might be Rick having changed his mind and now demanding that she return his dog to him. But instead it was Jeannie.

"Hi, kiddo; I thought it was about time for a check-up call. How's it going?"

"Okay." Claire yawned and pulled the quilt around her as she threw some sticks onto the embers.

"So, how's the painting coming along?"

"Pretty good, actually." Claire brightened, still not fully awake, but ready to tell Jeannie about her breakthrough. "You see, I got this dog named Michael—he's kind of like my angel, you know. Hey, isn't Michael an angel name? Like the one who protects or something? Or maybe that's Gabriel. Anyway, this guy's name is Michael." She walked over and opened the door to let the dog out.

"Well, good," Jeannie paused. "That sounds real good. But what about the painting?"

"That's what I'm trying to tell you, Jeannie. I've been able to paint again. I mean, ever since Michael came, I've been painting. First I thought I was just painting snow—everything was just white-white-white. Then I saw these angels—well, not actually saw them, I guess. But I dreamt them, and it felt real. And I thought, hey, those snowscapes just need some angels thrown in."

"Snowscapes? Angels?" Jeannie sounded skeptical.

"Oh, don't worry, they're not like cherubs or something you'd hang on your Christmas tree. And if you squint your eyes you almost can't see them—"

"Uh, what else have you done, Claire?"

"You mean besides angels?"

"Yeah. What else you got cooking?"

"Nothing really. Just angels. It's like I can't paint anything but angels and snow right now. I know it sounds weird, but I think it's a real breakthrough."

"Uh-huh."

"I can hear that sound in your voice, Jeannie." Claire took in a quick breath. "It's like you think I'm going wacko or something. And I have to admit I've had these same concerns myself—I mean especially when I started relating to how Vincent cut off his ear and everything—"

"Claire!"

"I'm sorry, Jeannie. I don't mean to sound crazy. And really, I'm just fine, really I am. I think this angel thing all started when I first saw those footprints in the snow. I mean they look exactly like Scott and Jeremy's, and I keep thinking maybe they're out here—just walking around in the—"

"That does it, Claire. I'm coming out."

"But you don't need—"

"Yes, I do. I need to do an ear count on you. And I don't even care what day it is."

"What day is it?"

"Oh, you poor thing. You don't even know what day it is? Why, it's Thanksgiving, of course."

"Thanksgiving?" Claire considered this.

"Yes. And I'm coming out. I'll even bring a turkey. And maybe some friends too. You ready for company?"

"Uh, well . . ." Claire looked around the small cabin, at herself still dressed in her rumpled clothes from the day before. "Yeah, sure. If you really want to—"

"I'll see you around two then. Don't do anything foolish before I get there."

Claire hung up the phone feeling slightly stunned. And she'd forgotten to warn Jeannie about the snow on the roads. She went to let Michael back inside and looked around. Fortunately, yesterday's sun had melted it down some, and it looked to be doing the same today. But was it really Thanksgiving? She scratched her head. How had she missed that? Maybe she really was going crazy. Oh, well, they always say you're the last one to find out.

8

Claire carefully stacked her paintings against the wall, then draped them with a sheet. It wasn't that she wanted to hide them exactly. And yet she wasn't eager to have them viewed either. Not by strangers certainly. Not even by Jeannie. Then she went to work preparing what she hoped would be some adequate side dishes to accompany Jeannie's turkey. Midway through the day she decided to call her dad. She knew he wasn't much into holidays, hadn't been since her mother died more than ten years ago.

"Hi, Daddy. Happy Thanksgiving."

"Hey, sweetie, how're you doing out there in the middle of nowhere's-ville?"

"I'm doing okay. I've been painting."

"Really? Good for you. Maybe you were right about needing all that isolation after all. Although I know I couldn't handle it myself. I needed you and all my friends around after I lost your mother."

"Well, I wouldn't want to live out here indefinitely. But for the time being, I think it's doing the trick."

"I'm glad to hear it. I've really been praying for you, Claire."

"Thanks, Daddy. I can tell that somebody has. So, you doing anything special for Thanksgiving?"

"Hank and I played eighteen holes this morning, and he's here right now trying to talk me into coming over to his place this afternoon, but I don't know."

"Oh, you should go, Daddy. Remember what you just said about needing your friends."

"Yeah, I suppose you're right. But what about you? You got any neighbors out there in the sticks wanting to eat turkey with you?"

"Actually, Jeannie's coming up. Maybe bringing some friends too."

"Well, good for Jeannie. She's a good ol' gal."

"Yeah." Claire glanced over at the shrouded canvases. "But I'm not sure that I want her to see my paintings just yet."

"Why's that?"

"Oh, I don't know. I guess I'm afraid she'll think they're weird. Or worse yet, she might think they're terrible and then be afraid to tell me for fear that I might completely fall apart and never paint again."

He laughed. "I've never known Jeannie to be anything but honest. And why would she think they're weird?"

"They have angels in them, Daddy."

"Angels?"

Claire bit her lip and waited.

"Well, what's wrong with angels anyway? Lots of Renaissance painters painted angels, didn't they?"

"Yeah. But my style isn't exactly Renaissance, you know, it's more impressionistic. And I can't think of too many impressionists who were into angels."

He chuckled. "Maybe it's time for a first. I think it sounds great, Claire. If you want to paint angels, you just go ahead and paint angels. And if Jeannie can't sell them, well then, I'll buy one, and I'll bet Hank will too. Right, Hank?"

"Oh, I forgot you have Hank there, Daddy. I better get back to my kitchen work anyway. Give him my love, and Marie too."

"You bet. Now you have a good day, sweetheart. And don't worry about those angels; if you don't want to show them to anyone yet, then don't."

She set down the phone and went back to her cooking. It was a challenge to make anything too festive with her spartan ingredients, but then she wasn't an artist for nothing. By two o'clock she had concocted an apple pie with a festively decorated crust complete with sculpted pastry leaves (hopefully it would taste as good as it looked). And she put together a pretty looking cheese and cracker plate, even if it only contained three ordinary types of cheeses cut into interesting shapes. What she lacked in food variety she hoped to make up for with ingenuity. She even managed to put together a centerpiece using pinecones, juniper berries, moss, and some emergency candles. And it wasn't half bad, although she knew the candles wouldn't last long once lit.

As it turned out, Jeannie only managed to entice one friend to drive up the mountain pass with her, her old friend Leo Goldberg. Claire only knew Leo casually, as someone loosely connected with the art world in the Bay Area and someone Jeannie had dated off and on over the past few years but had never seemed terribly serious about.

"Claire, you look lovely," said Leo as they walked in the door. Then after setting a large cardboard box on the table, he took both her hands in his. "The mountain air must agree with you."

"Yes," agreed Jeannie as she removed her big wool cape and gave Claire a kiss. "You've even got roses in your cheeks."

Claire smiled. "Oh, I'm so glad you came up, Jeannie."

"Well, to be honest, I was worried you might be up here gnawing on a table leg and mumbling to yourself."

"Yes, she was beside herself thinking you might've lopped off an ear." Leo looked at her carefully. "But they both appear to be intact."

Claire forced an awkward smile. "Actually, that might not be too far from the truth." She patted the dog's head. "But this guy has been good company for me."

"Okay, let's get this turkey into the oven to heat," said Jeannie. "And then I want to see those paintings."

"Did you actually cook this?" Claire opened the oven door and slid the golden brown turkey inside.

Jeannie laughed. "Are you kidding? I'm a city girl, and I know how to survive in the city—it's called take-out."

Leo began unpacking other food items, and he and Jeannie continued to laugh and joke about her lack of culinary skills. But suddenly the cabin began to feel overly full and slightly stuffy to Claire. She found herself stepping away from them. And she felt relieved that Jeannie had brought only one friend.

"Do you guys want to take a walk before dinner?" she asked, longing for fresh air and hoping to distract them from wanting to see her art just yet.

"Hmmm?" Jeannie looked outside the window and tapped the toe of her soft leather high-heeled boots. "I didn't exactly wear hiking boots, if you know what I mean."

"Right." Claire pointed to the chairs at the maple table. "Why don't you both sit down? Would you like some coffee or tea? I have hot water all ready."

"Tea sounds lovely." Jeannie sat down at the table, but Claire saw her eyeing the draped canvases off to her right.

Claire poured the hot water into the teapot, breathing deeply as she gazed out the window above the sink, willing herself to relax.

"Those your paintings?" asked Jeannie, as stubborn as ever.

Claire waited while the tea steeped in the pot before she returned to the table. "Yeah. But I'm not sure they're ready to be—"

"Jeannie says you've been painting angels." Leo leaned back in his chair and crossed his leg, an unreadable expression across his face. "I suppose you haven't heard that the angel trend is over now."

"Oh, Leo." Jeannie frowned and waved her hand. "Angels have been around forever."

Claire sat down with them and poured tea. "So, do you mean to say that you believe in them too, Jeannie?"

Jeannie laughed. "I *mean* that they've been represented in various art forms for thousands of years. Good grief, you can probably find them carved into some cave walls from prehistoric times. So they're certainly not only a modern-day fad, although Leo's right," she cleared her throat, "our latest angel trend is probably over by now. But that shouldn't matter—not really." Still there was something unconvincing in Jeannie's voice, like she was only trying to humor Claire.

"Cheese and crackers?" Claire hopped up to get the platter she'd so carefully prepared earlier.

"Very pretty," said Leo as he took one.

"Well, I didn't really shop for Thanksgiving," she admitted. "My pantry was a little, shall we say, boring, so I thought I better at least try to make it look good."

"But back to the paintings." Jeannie nodded toward the canvases again. "You don't really want to keep me in suspense like this, do you?"

Claire smiled. "Actually, I do."

Jeannie leaned her head back and groaned. "Whatever for?"

"Well, I'd like to enjoy your company and the dinner before . . ."

"Before what?" asked Leo.

"She's afraid we're going to hate them." Jeannie shrugged. "Well, even if they're not very good, Claire, at least you are painting. That's the main thing. And you've only been up here—what? A few weeks now. There's time to do more. I know how fast you work once you get going." She winked at Leo. "That's one thing I love about my impressionists, they usually work in a whirlwind of inspiration—producing a volume of paintings in a short amount of time."

Claire glanced at Leo. "Forgive me, Leo, but I've forgotten exactly what your connection to the art world is."

He grinned. "You may be sorry you asked."

Jeannie rolled her eyes. "Claire, honestly!"

He waved his hand. "Oh, it's all right, Jeannie—"

"No, Claire should know better than this. For heaven's sake, Leo is an art critic with the *Times*."

Claire slapped her forehead. "Oh, that's right. I'm sorry. But Jeannie can vouch for the fact that I go out of my way to remain oblivious in that area. I'm that proverbial ostrich with my head—well, who knows where? I just don't pay much attention to the reviews. I figure if someone praised my work I might turn into a prima donna and sit around on my laurels all day. And, on the other hand, if someone criticizes my work, I'm sure to take it personally and never want to paint again. And I've already been creatively paralyzed for over a year now. So, for me, it's better not to know. Besides I trust that Jeannie's keeping up with all that, and she sort of lets me know, gently, how I'm being received out there."

Leo ran his fingers down his goatee beard. "Then you probably want me to keep my mouth shut if I take a peek at your work today?"

Claire sighed. "I don't know. I probably don't really want anyone to look at it just yet."

"Come on," said Jeannie. "You can't possibly think I'd drive all the way up here and then leave without even looking."

"I thought you said this was a mental health visit," teased Claire.

Leo laughed. "Yes, and I also heard you've been chasing angels in the woods."

Claire looked down at the table.

"I'm sorry," said Leo. "I didn't mean to—"

"Oh, come on," urged Jeannie. "Claire isn't as thin-skinned as that. Are you, Claire?"

Claire looked up. "No. But you're right, Leo. I have been chasing angels in the woods."

"Well, good for you." He clapped his hands. "I like an artist with spirit and passion. It's always sure to show through in their work."

"So, you don't think I'm crazy? I mean, did Jeannie tell you that I found footprints and that I thought they belonged to my deceased husband and son—or maybe angels?"

He smiled. "Yes. I think it's a charming story. And who are we to say what's real and what's not? If it seems real to you—"

"Enough!" Jeannie stood up. "Please, don't encourage her along these lines, Leo. Claire's been through a lot this past year. She needs to move on now."

"But perhaps this is part of the moving on process for her," he argued. "Maybe she needs to chase angels in the woods to escape something. Maybe it's how she'll become free of her grief. Who are we to say?"

Jeannie sat down again. "Oh, I don't know. I just want to see her get better. And all this talk of angels-angels-angels . . . frankly it worries me."

Claire reached over and patted Jeannie's hand. "I appreciate your concern. To be honest, it worries me a little too. Sometimes, in the middle of the day when I'm doing something ordinary like heating soup or feeding the dog, I think all my obsession with angels is pure nonsense. But then, at other times, like in the silence of the snowy woods, or in the middle of the night . . . well, I'm not so sure."

"A lot of people believe in angels," said Leo quietly. "There are all kinds of books written about them."

"You two." Jeannie pressed her lips together and shook her head.

"Have you read any books on angels, Leo?" Claire leaned forward, eager to hear anything he had to say on the subject.

"No, but my mother has. She happens to be a devout believer in angels."

Claire sighed. "It's encouraging to know I'm not alone."

"Come now," said Jeannie. "It worries me to think of you out there in the snow trying to track down your dead husband and son—forgive me for being so blunt, Claire. But it sounds pretty outrageous to me."

"Oh, I don't really think it's them. . . ." She gazed out the window with a longing to be out there, walking in the cool snow.

"But you *want* it to be," said Jeannie. "That's almost as bad."

"Of course, she wants it to be them," defended Leo. "Who wouldn't want to see their departed loved ones again, if they could?"

Claire nodded. "But at the same time, I know I need to let them go. I know I need to accept that those footprints out there probably don't really belong to them."

"*Probably?*" Jeannie lifted an eyebrow.

"Okay, they *don't* belong to them."

"That's better." Jeannie glanced up at the clock. "I'll bet that turkey's almost heated by now. We should warm up those potatoes and gravy and rolls too."

The three of them enjoyed a homey and delicious dinner, and Michael enjoyed the treats tossed his way from the table. Then Jeannie helped clean up while Claire made coffee to go with their pie. Finally, they were all sitting at the table, leaning back in their chairs and feeling stuffed and content.

"It's times like this when I wish I still smoked my pipe," said Leo as he patted his full midsection.

Jeannie stood and walked slowly over to the paintings. "The time has come, Claire. Are you ready?"

Claire took in a deep breath. "Are you two ready?"

Leo rubbed his hands together. "Well, if anticipation has anything to do with it, you've sure got me going, Claire."

Claire walked over to the paintings, wondering about the best way to do this. "All right," she finally said, "if we're going to have an art show, you need to give me a couple of minutes to set up, okay?"

"Maybe we should step outside for a breath of fresh air," suggested Leo.

"Good idea," said Claire. "I'm sure Michael would enjoy stretching his legs a bit too."

With the cabin to herself, Claire rearranged the table and chairs and lights to best accommodate and display her work. She set four of the paintings on the chairs and finally placed the picture of Scott and Jeremy on the easel, draping it with the sheet, still unwilling to show it to anyone. Then she went outside to invite them back in.

Her voice actually trembled as she spoke. "Okay, the gallery is officially open."

"I'm so excited," said Leo. And that alone filled Claire with dread. An art critic! What had Jeannie been thinking?

Claire lurked behind them as they entered the cabin. She stood silently as they viewed the works, watching their every move, waiting for their reactions. But Jeannie and Leo said nothing—absolutely nothing. They simply moved about the crowded space, situating themselves to best view her various works.

"Perhaps if they were framed," she finally said weakly, almost inaudibly.

The floor squeaked beneath Leo as he moved to get a better look at the night painting. His hands hung loosely at his sides. But still he said nothing.

"Oh, I should've known," muttered Claire. "I never should've. . . ." She walked over to the sink and stared blankly out the window, wishing desperately that her company would just quietly turn and leave. Or perhaps she could leave, maybe just vanish into the air, like an angel.

Finally, Jeannie spoke, but her voice was different somehow; perhaps it was strained by all this. "What's under this, Claire?" She was standing before the easel now.

Claire stepped up to the easel. Well, why not get it over with. She might as well let them see it all. Like a felon about to be sentenced, she pulled the sheet from the painting, then stepped back, unable to actually look at it herself. Oh, if only this cabin had another room, besides the bathroom, where she might run and hide. She felt her teeth clenching and wished that this day could be over— that Jeannie and Leo could politely excuse themselves and get in Jeannie's BMW and just leave. But still they stood there, just looking in silence. As if they were too embarrassed to speak. And Claire felt as if she were standing before the two of them naked and ashamed, with nowhere to hide.

At last Jeannie turned around and faced her. But her expression was confusing. Was she upset? Angry? Frustrated by Claire's lame excuse for art? Then Claire noticed there were real tears in Jeannie's eyes.

Jeannie pulled out a handkerchief and daubed at her eyes. "These are beautiful, Claire."

"Really?" Claire grabbed Jeannie by the arms. "Tell me the truth, Jeannie. Are you just saying that? Are you afraid I've totally lost it, gone off the deep end, and you don't want to tell me for fear I'll completely crack up, and you'll have to get the men in the white coats and—"

"No!" Jeannie leaned forward and looked directly into Claire's eyes. "I *mean* it. I'm perfectly serious. These are the best things you've ever done."

Now Claire felt tears filling her own eyes. "What about you, Leo?" she asked in a shaky voice. "What do you think?"

He turned around to face her. His expression was still impossible to read, but if anything he looked slightly frightened.

"Are you okay?" she asked, stepping closer.

He nodded and took a deep breath. "You really want my opinion, Claire? Despite what you said earlier about critics?"

She considered this, then nodded. "Yes. Tell me the truth."

"These are brilliant." He rubbed his goatee thoughtfully. "I can't even think of the right words to describe them—and I'm a writer—inspired, holy, powerful, inspirational, amazing . . . that's just for starters."

She felt her knees growing weak and eased herself down into the easy chair, placing her head in her hands as she sobbed in pure relief. She felt both of them near her, their hands resting on her shoulders as they waited for this moment to pass. Finally, she looked up at them and asked, "Are you guys telling me the truth? *For real?*"

They both nodded.

"I have to take these with me, Claire. Henri must see them at once. If it's at all possible, we have to get a show scheduled before Christmas, even if that means moving some things around. Do you think you'll have any more done by then?"

"I–I don't know. It's like they come to me—like Leo said—in inspiration. Like God is actually guiding my hand."

"I believe that," said Leo.

Jeannie nodded. "Well, whatever it takes, if you can do more, it'll help the show."

"Are you sure, Jeannie? I mean, like Leo said, angels aren't really in vogue right now. And what if Henri doesn't—"

"You let me figure this out."

"But you really think anyone would want to buy them?"

Jeannie pressed her lips together. "Well, you can just never tell about these things. I've seen work that I thought was amazing and brilliant before, but the public just didn't seem to get it. I suppose that could happen."

Leo nodded thoughtfully. "Yes, I've seen it too. I've given artists the best reviews and then watched them sink into oblivion."

Claire looked down at her lap. "Yeah, I know what you mean."

"But we've got to give it a try," said Jeannie. She glanced at her watch. "And we should probably be on our way now, Claire."

Claire stood and took Jeannie's hand. "Thanks so much for everything."

"I'll load up the pictures," said Leo. "Do you have any spare blankets to wrap them in?"

"There are some in that closet by the bathroom," instructed Jeannie.

"The one on the easel . . ." Claire began with hesitation.

"Yes?" Jeannie nodded.

"I don't really want to sell that one."

"I didn't think you would." Jeannie put her hand on Claire's shoulder. "But can you let it be in the show?"

Claire glanced over at the painting, knowing she would miss it but also knowing it might be better to have it away from her, for now. "Yes. You can take it."

"Good."

After the paintings were loaded, Jeannie turned to Claire. "About those footprints in the woods?"

"Yes?"

"Well, maybe they are something more. I mean, you never know."

Claire smiled. "Or maybe you're just saying that because you like the inspiration they provided."

Jeannie grinned. "Maybe."

"So you like representing a mad artist, now, do you?"

Jeannie shook her head. "No. I like representing *you*. I definitely do *not* want you to go mad. And if necessary, I recommend you search out those footprints if only to prove to yourself they belong to a couple of perfectly normal human beings just out enjoying nature the same as you."

"Yes, I may do that."

"I just want you to stay healthy, kiddo." Then Jeannie leaned over and gave her a kiss on the cheek. "You take care of yourself now. And don't you quit believing in angels!"

"That's right," called Leo. "I can't wait to tell my mom about you!"

9

For the next two weeks, Claire divided her time between painting and walking and daily chores, all this with Michael by her side. Painting came more easily to her now; it almost seemed that something new had been unleashed or maybe broken when Claire heard the approval of two art professionals. And it wasn't that her art was dependent on the opinions of others, but under the circumstances, she appreciated it.

She had suspected she wouldn't be able to keep up the frenzied, somewhat crazed pace of her original angel pieces. But she'd known even then that it was slightly fanatical, almost over the edge. Now she was thankful to simply continue. Plus she noticed that a quiet peace seemed to accompany her as she worked. And to Jeannie's great pleasure, Claire managed to create four more paintings for the show. She could hardly contain herself as she told Jeannie the good news on the phone.

"I can't wait to see them," exclaimed Jeannie. "I'll send a courier to pick them up. If I get right on it, he could be there by late this afternoon."

"They're a lot like the earliest ones," explained Claire as she studied her latest painting. "Mostly shades of white on white and snow-covered trees with angels here and there. Sometimes I worry that the angels are too subtle; I'm afraid the viewer could almost miss them."

"Yeah, but once they see them, they'd wonder how they ever missed them in the first place."

"I hope you're right." Claire said, washing out a dirty brush.

"Of course, I'm right. Everything's all set too. The show will begin this weekend. Did I tell you that Henri actually postponed an *Andrew Banks* show until *after* the New Year—can you believe it? Just so he could squeeze your show in *before* Christmas. He's such a doll. And he plans to run it for three weeks—it's his best-selling season of the year, you know. Can you believe our luck with this timing?"

Claire bit into her lip. "I just hope he's not disappointed."

"What do you mean?"

"I mean it could be a total flop."

"Well, you let us worry about that, kiddo. You just keep on chasing those amazing angels."

Claire sighed. "That's got me worried."

"What's wrong, sweetie?"

"Well, I've been having those old dreams again. And I can't quit thinking about those—those footprints in the snow. I know it sounds crazy, Jeannie, and I don't really believe it right now, but sometimes in the middle of the night, I feel just certain that they belong to Scott and Jeremy."

"Claire, you know it can't really be—"

"Oh, I know, I know—at least my head knows, most of the time anyway. But it's this whole angel thing that's got me going. And strange things have happened to other people. Lucy at the store was telling me just yesterday that a friend of hers is certain he saw Big Foot a few years ago. So how can I be so certain that it isn't them? What if it is?"

Jeannie exhaled loudly. "Well, as your rep, I shouldn't even say this—it's like shooting myself in the foot—or telling you to kill off your muse . . . but as your friend I know I have to speak up." She cleared her throat. "Claire, it's like I said before, I think it's time you followed those footprints—to their final conclusion, I mean. Then, and only then, you will see that they belong to a pair of perfectly ordinary human beings—flesh and blood . . . not feathers and angel dust. Come to think of it, it could be the old couple that has a place down the road a ways. They used to walk pretty regularly as I recall. I think their name was Henson or Henderson. And she was a real tiny lady; I'll bet she could have child-sized feet."

"Yeah, you're probably right." Claire considered an older couple walking through the snowy woods. Yes, it could happen. "I've tried to follow the footprints before, but for one reason or another, I always turned back. Lately I've been thinking about following them again, but. . . ." She paused, uncertain.

"The illusion would be over."

Claire swallowed. "Yeah. That's what I'm thinking."

"Well, maybe it's time to end this thing—to really move on, you know? I realize that life dealt you a really low blow in losing Scott and Jeremy. But you've got a bright future, kiddo. And there are all kinds of good things in store for you, but you need to be ready for them. And even if this means it's the end of your—uh—angel era, I'm sure you'll still be inspired to paint something else equally wonderful, in time. Talent like yours doesn't come along every day."

Claire was ready for this conversation to end. "I hope you're right, Jeannie; I want to believe you."

"Trust me, sweetie, it's not healthy for you to live in a fantasy world." She paused, then laughed. "And as greedy as I am to have you producing more of those lovely angel paintings, I'm not willing to see you sacrifice your emotional well-being for them."

"Thanks. I appreciate your honesty."

"And, don't forget, I want you here for the opening of the show."

"What day is that again?"

"This Friday night. Come at seven for the preview showing. I have some people I want you to meet. Shall I send someone for you?"

"No. I can drive. I'm just not sure what to do about Michael."

"Michael?"

"My dog."

"Oh, yeah. Why not bring him along?"

"I would, except the landlord doesn't allow pets in my apartment."

"Oh." She could hear Jeannie tapping her pencil on the phone now, her sign that it was time to hang up. "Well, you know I'm not crazy about dogs, but I suppose he could stay at my place."

"Thanks, Jeannie. I might have to take you up on that."

"See you on Friday then.

After another restless night, haunted by the same old dream, Claire decided that Jeannie was right. It was time to follow those footprints and just get it over with. And, after all, why shouldn't she become acquainted with her neighbors, the Hendersons, or whoever they were. If they were real neighbors, that is.

"Ready for a nice long walk?" she asked Michael after putting away the last of the breakfast dishes.

He wagged his tail in response and waited by the door as she slowly bundled up. Several inches of fresh snow had fallen the night before, and the temperature had dropped since yesterday. She took a few minutes to stack more firewood on the porch, then the two of them set out. As she walked, she wondered if she shouldn't just pack things up this week. Hadn't she accomplished what she'd set out to do? To break the bond that had kept her from painting? What other reason was there to stay? She looked at Michael happily running ahead of her. That "no dog" policy at her loft apartment did present a bit of a problem, but perhaps she could sublet it and find a new place. But where?

She shook her head, as if to dispose of these troubling thoughts. Why not just enjoy the day, the walk, the snow? After all, if she decided to stay in San Francisco after the opening, it could be her last chance to be here and to do this. She took in a deep breath and looked up at the sky. She hadn't noticed earlier that it had that heavy look again—that dull gray density that could possibly mean more snow. Hopefully it would hold off until later that afternoon. By then she'd have met the old couple and be safely back at her cabin, probably packing up to leave. She'd have to remember to take some time to stop by and say good-bye to old Lucy. Lucy had been a real godsend, especially when it came to securing the deal with Michael. Claire smiled to herself as she recalled Lucy's surprised face when she'd gone in to settle up Rick's bill for the dog. Claire had painted a small angel picture for her on an old piece of board she'd found in the shed. Nothing really special, but Lucy had been deeply touched.

"I'll hang it right here by the cash register," she'd promised. "Why, it's my first piece of honest to goodness art—and from a real live artist too!"

Claire and Michael trekked through the woods until they reached the dead tree. And there, to her surprise, were two sets of fresh tracks, clearly visible, as if they'd just been made. This was more than she'd hoped for! She'd expected to at least discover some old tracks that were still discernable, but nothing as plain as these. She looked up the trail, half expecting to see an old couple slowly walking along. But there was no one. Still, she should have no problem following these footprints to their "final conclusion," as Jeannie had put it. And if she hurried she might actually catch up with them.

She walked fast. Pausing at the footbridge to catch her breath, she glanced up at the sky with slight apprehension. The clouds seemed a little lower now, but no flakes were falling as yet. Still she could never be sure. "Okay, boy, ready to go?"

Michael turned around as if to head back toward home as usual. "No, we're going this way today, Michael," Claire said.

He looked at her curiously, then joined her, tail wagging eagerly.

"Yes, we're going to meet our neighbors," she announced as they continued on, her heart beating a little faster in anticipation.

After about ten minutes of fast walking, Claire noticed it had begun to snow. Nothing threatening, just a few random flakes. But the farther she got from the turning point of the footbridge, the more her heart began to pound. What in the world was she doing? And why? Tracking footprints that belonged to a couple of old-timers? What did she really hope to prove by this anyway? And what if the footprints simply went on and on —traveling off into nowhere? What if she and Michael were to become lost out here, all alone in the wilderness with no one for miles around? Who would ever think to check on them or go out to look? She stopped and glanced nervously at the trail behind her. Should she turn back? It wasn't too late to stop and retrace her steps. And yet something beyond herself, something deep within, seemed to drive and compel her forward. And so she continued, praying silently as she went.

The footprints continued up over a slight hill, then curved off to the right. The snow was falling harder as she and Michael descended the hill, and she could feel it blowing around her in little flurries. And visibility began to decrease.

"It can't be too far ahead," she said aloud, to assure herself as much as Michael. She noticed that the footprints were becoming less distinct; they were slowly being devoured by the quickly falling snow. "We've got to hurry, Michael!"

Claire began to jog, keeping her eyes focused on the ground ahead of her, afraid if she made one wrong turn, she and Michael might be lost out here forever. She paused once to look behind her. At least her freshly made footprints were still fairly clear; she ought to be able to follow them home if weather forced them to turn back. She tried to envision the older couple out walking in the snow. But somehow it just didn't fit. And then she remembered the pair of snow angels—one big, one small. Surely an elderly couple wouldn't lie down on the snow and make snow angels—would they? And if the rapidly fading footprints in front of her didn't belong to that elderly couple, whom did they belong to? Could it be?

She continued jogging, a tight feeling wrapping itself around her chest with each step. The snow was falling even faster now, and the trail was a blur. She couldn't even be sure she was still following the footprints. Perhaps she had stumbled onto a deer trail. She knew how they crisscrossed the National Forest. A person could become lost for weeks following such a trail.

"Oh, dear God," she cried out breathlessly as she continued pressing on. "Help me!"

Finally, she stopped running and bent over, her chest heaving up and down from the exertion. She wasn't even sure how long she'd been traveling, but a knifelike pain stabbed into her right side, and her lungs burned like fire. She knew she could run no farther. Her legs felt like lead, and her heart was consumed with fear. She knew she was lost. And all around her was white and swirling snow, thick and opaque, like a living blanket that wanted to suffocate her. She looked all around, unable to see her dog.

"*Michael!*" she screamed. But her voice sounded dull, hushed by the deadening acoustics of the snow and the wind. "Michael!" she cried again, turning around in a circle. "Please, come here, boy!"

10

Claire never knew for sure how she got there. Perhaps it was like in her angel dream, with a pair of invisible celestial beings lifting her up and carrying her along, high above the storm. Or maybe it was Michael, her angel dog, who had led her to safety. She could only imagine. But somehow, both she and her faithful companion emerged half frozen from the snowy woods. And seeing a faint golden light up ahead, she stumbled stubbornly toward it, forcing one icy foot in front of the other until she collapsed on the porch of a cabin not much larger than her own.

And even then she couldn't remember anyone coming to the door, or opening it up and saying, "Hello, and what have we here?" In fact, she later learned she had never even made it to the door. It was Michael's persistent scratching and loud barks that had finally aroused the attention of the tenants. The first thing Claire remembered was sitting in front of the big river rock fireplace, her bare feet wrapped in a soft woolen throw, and a young girl, about age ten, Claire guessed, holding a thick mug of hot tea before her.

"Can you drink this?" asked the girl in a quiet voice.

"Thank you." Claire believed she said those words, although she couldn't be sure. But she did recall taking the warm mug into her hands and eagerly wrapping her cold fingers around its exterior, then slowly drinking the hot contents.

"My dad's calling for help," said the girl.

Claire felt her eyes open more widely. "Help?"

"For you. He thinks you have hyperthermia."

Claire thought she may have smiled at that. "You mean hypothermia?"

The girl solemnly nodded. "You looked frozen."

"My dog?" Suddenly Claire remembered being unable to see Michael in the snow. The girl pointed to her left and, curled right next to Claire's bundled feet, Michael rested by the warmth of the fire.

"He's okay." The girl ran her hand along Michael's still damp coat. "He's a good dog, isn't he?"

Claire nodded. "Thank you for helping us. My name is Claire. I live in a cabin—"

"Has she come to?" This came from a male voice, and he sounded worried. Claire turned to see a man now entering the room. His blond hair looked disheveled and his beard in need of a trim. "Are you okay?" He came over and knelt in front of Claire, peering into her eyes as if to discern her mental stability as much as her physical well-being.

"I think I'm fine," she answered, feeling like the village idiot. "I—uh—got lost in the snow."

"I can understand that," he said, standing to peer out the window. "It's turned into a real blizzard out there."

"I'm sorry to trouble you—"

"Good grief, you're no trouble. You and your dog looked like you were about to freeze out there."

"I'm so glad we stumbled onto your house."

"I'll say. You must've had a guardian angel watching over you."

She looked at him closely. "An angel?"

He laughed. "Well, who knows? But how are you feeling now? It doesn't look like you're suffering from frostbite. Fortunately you were well bundled up. But I suspect you worked up a sweat trying to find your way through the snow, and you were getting pretty chilled."

She nodded, noticing now that her heavy wool jacket had been replaced by a thick polar-fleece blanket. "Yes, we were running—I got scared—"

"I was afraid you might have hypothermia. You were shivering pretty badly. I called 911, and they told me just to get you warm and that it would take them at least two hours to get anyone out here, due to the weather."

"Oh, I don't need anyone—"

"Right, I'll let them know."

"I'm actually starting to feel warmer now." She looked up into his eyes, noticing that they were a mixture of blue and gray and perhaps a mossy green. Interesting really. "I should probably get going."

He laughed. "Not in this weather, you don't."

She looked out at the snow still swirling in menacing circles. "I suppose you're right."

"We'll give you a ride home as soon as you've had a chance to get thoroughly warm and when the weather abates some."

"Thanks." She looked over at the girl who was still peering at her curiously. "Thanks for everything."

"It was your dog that got Anna's attention." He nodded to the girl. "He was scratching and barking. Pretty smart dog, that one."

Michael opened his eyes and looked up now, his tail thumping on the floor.

She reached down to pat his head. "Good boy, Michael."

"Michael?" said the girl. "Is that his name?"

"Yes," Claire answered her then looked back at the man. "And as I was just telling your—uh, your daughter?"

He nodded. "That's right."

"That my name is Claire Andrews, and I live in a cabin over on Ridge Road."

"I'm Garret Henderson—"

"Oh, are your parents the Hendersons—" she interrupted, then laughed. "I mean do they own this place? My friend mentioned an older couple named—"

"Yes, Marge and Carl. They stay here during the warmer months. But usually this place is abandoned in winter."

Anna nodded. "You're lucky we were here."

"I'll say."

"What I can't figure out is what you were doing this far from home." Garret scratched his already messy hair. "And in weather like this."

"I know. I must seem like a crazy woman to be out in this." She frowned. "Actually, it's kind of a long story."

"And you should probably rest." Garret stepped back. "And I need to call those 911 folks back and let them know we don't need an ambulance or anything."

"Right." Claire leaned her head back into the comfortable chair and closed her eyes. She felt so silly about her quest now—trekking off in the middle of a snowstorm to find her lost angels. Good grief, had she been mad? And, of course, Jeannie had been right. Two perfectly normal human beings. No feathers or angel dust anywhere.

"More tea?" offered Anna.

Claire opened her eyes to see Anna with her hand out, ready to take the nearly empty mug. The girl had a lovely oval-shaped face with clear blue eyes. Her hair, slightly darker than her father's, was about the color of polished oak. "Thank you," said Claire, "more tea would be nice."

When Anna returned, Claire asked her how old she was.

"I'll be eleven next month," she said proudly.

Claire nodded. "That was about my guess."

"I'm really supposed to be in school right now, but I got special permission to be with my dad while he works on his book."

"His book?"

"Yeah." Anna smiled brightly. "My dad is an author."

"Cool." Claire took a sip of tea. She wanted to ask about Anna's mother but couldn't quite put this question into words, at least not into words that didn't sound rude or intrusive.

"We've been here since school started in September. I'm doing home school until we go back and I can be in my class again." She frowned.

"And you're not looking forward to that?"

"Not really. I like it out here. And I think I learn more doing home school than I do at real school. My dad's a good teacher."

"What kind of books does your dad write?"

"Novels." Anna's eyes grew wide. "That means they're fiction, which is the same as not being true. Oh, it's not that my dad tells lies, but he makes his stories up, you know?"

Claire smiled. "Yes, I know."

"Actually, he writes historical novels."

A light went on. "Does your dad go by the name of G. A. Henderson?"

"Yeah. Garret Allen Henderson." She nodded proudly. "That's him."

"I've read some of his books. He's good."

Anna's face grew brighter than ever, and suddenly Claire wished she could paint her. She would be a perfect model for an angel. Not that Claire had needed models before, but the idea appealed to her now.

"Well, I think I finally convinced them that you were okay," said Garret, coming back into the room. "But they were pretty determined to send out an ambulance."

"I'm sorry to cause so much trouble."

"Oh, it's okay. I think I needed a break anyway."

"Yeah, he has barely stopped working today," complained Anna.

"She told me that you're an author," said Claire. "I've actually read a few of your books—and liked them."

He smiled—kind of a crooked smile but sincere, and nice. "Thanks. I guess you'd have to say that though, wouldn't you. You wouldn't want to risk me throwing you back out in the freezing snow again."

She laughed. "No, really. I did like them. You're very good."

He shook his head. "Well, I'm not so sure about that anymore. It's taken me nearly two years to finish this last one, and even now, I'm . . ." He sighed deeply. "Well, just not too sure."

"I'll bet it's the best thing you've ever done."

He looked at her curiously. "Don't know what makes you think so. But let's hope you're right."

"Well, I think we sometimes become the most critical of our work when it's really the best."

"Are you a writer?"

She smiled. "No. Actually I'm an artist."

"*An artist?*" Anna's eyes grew wide. "A *real* artist?"

"Oh, no." Garret held his hands in mock alarm. "Now, you've gone and done it. You didn't realize that Anna is absolutely enamored by artists. She'll probably never let you go home now."

Claire laughed. "A girl after my own heart. Well, don't worry, Anna, I used to be just like that too. That is, until I got to meet way too many artists. Although I must admit I still get giddy sometimes when I meet someone I really admire."

"Yeah," said Garret. "I'm like that too—with authors."

"What kind of art do you do?" Anna asked eagerly.

"Maybe I should leave you girls on your own for a while," said Garret. "Perhaps I can finish this chapter up before I take you home. I was just getting into the groove, you know, before you got here."

"Of course," Claire waved her hand. "I absolutely understand. I'm the same way with my art."

For the next hour, Claire and Anna talked about art. And Anna shyly showed her own sketches and watercolors, which Claire actually thought were quite well done for a girl that age—and told her so. Then Claire helped Anna prepare a light lunch of soup and grilled cheese sandwiches.

"I can cook almost anything," said Anna as she set the plate of sandwiches on the table.

"I believe it." Claire nodded. "You look like you know your way around the kitchen."

"Do I smell something?" Garret poked his head out from what Claire suspected was both an office and bedroom, since the cabin hadn't appeared large enough to have more than two bedrooms, plus the loft above.

"Just in time," said Anna. "We might've eaten them all up without you." She grinned at him. "Since I know you didn't want to be disturbed."

They all sat down at the table, then Garret and Anna bowed their heads to pray. Claire followed suit, both pleased and surprised by the gesture. After Garret said a quick but earnest sounding prayer, they all began to eat.

"Claire told me that she's been painting pictures of angels lately," Anna informed her father.

"I'd invite Anna to see them," explained Claire, "but they were just picked up yesterday for an art show this coming weekend."

"Where's the show?" asked Garret as he dipped his spoon into his soup.

"A gallery called The Blue Moon. It's in San Francisco."

"Hey, I know where that is," said Garret. "That's a pretty swanky joint."

"Henri LaFollete is the owner—and a friend of mine."

"Lucky you."

Claire considered his words without responding. "I told Anna I wished that I could paint her."

"Could she, Daddy?"

He frowned slightly. "I guess so; I mean, if she really wants to."

"Yes, I'd love to." Suddenly Claire remembered how her time in the mountains seemed to be coming to an end this week, how she'd been considering returning to the city for good on Thursday. "I guess I should say if I come back, that is."

"*If* you come back?" Anna frowned. "You mean you're leaving? I just barely get to meet my first real live artist and now you're leaving me? Already?"

"Hey, Anna, you don't want to make our guest feel—"

"Oh, it's okay. I can understand how she feels." Claire turned to Anna. "I'm not completely sure about leaving. I've still got some things to work out. For one thing, I'm not allowed to keep a dog in my apartment in the city. And I can't bear to part with Michael—"

"We could take care of him for you," said Anna eagerly. "I'd love to have a dog for a while. I'd take him for walks and brush him and everything."

Claire glanced uncomfortably at Garret who seemed to be remaining fairly silent just now. "Oh, I couldn't impose," she said. "First of all, I land on your doorstep in the midst of a blizzard, and then to leave my dog while I'm gone—"

"Oh, please," begged Anna the way only a ten-year-old can. "Can we take care of Michael? Please, Daddy?"

Garret cleared his throat and daubed his mouth with a napkin. "You'll have to let me think about this, Anna."

"But, Daddy—"

He stood. "Please, Anna. We'll discuss it later."

11

Later that evening, Claire wondered if she hadn't simply imagined the events of the day. And that strange but unforgettable encounter with Garret and Anna—perhaps she'd simply dreamed it. She busied herself with packing up her art supplies. Then, just as she closed the big wooden case, she wondered if she was really ready to leave yet. She looked over to where Michael was sleeping soundly by the fire—surely exhausted from his freezing trek through the woods today—proof that perhaps it was real after all. She knew she could take him to San Francisco with her, leave him with Jeannie, and begin searching for a new place that allowed dogs. But she couldn't erase the sound of Anna's voice, pleading to keep the dog for her. Surely the girl was a bit lonely, staying out here with only her father for company. And while Garret seemed a nice man, on first acquaintance anyway, he did appear slightly moody.

What had started out for her as a magical visit had eventually deteriorated into what felt like a hastily ended intrusion (of course, she'd been the intruder).

She'd almost considered inviting them into her cabin, to give Anna a close-up look at the life of a "real artist." Not that it was anything terribly interesting, but the girl had seemed so completely fascinated by it all. But after the way Garret had suddenly turned quite chilly toward her, all she could think of was escaping him and his unreadable scrutiny. If that's what it really was. And she couldn't even be sure of that. It was quite possible that she was just overreacting to everything, due to life in general plus her isolation of late. Perhaps she'd simply misplaced or forgotten all her previous social skills.

She realized now that she'd been pacing back and forth, completely unsettled by all this. And perhaps, if she were to be truly honest with herself, she could face the real reason for her unrest. Maybe the most disturbing part of her day was that she never did find Scott and Jeremy at the end of the trail. And she never stumbled across angels either. Well, at least not that she could remember. But then, who knew what may have accompanied her through the snowy woods, guiding her to safety. Still, it didn't matter. For, somehow, she knew that the events of the day were meant to force her to let go—to accept that Scott and Jeremy were gone now. And she would not see them again until it was time for her to leave this earth permanently too. She considered how close she may have been to actually joining them today and shuddered. Surprisingly, she was relieved to be alive. She wrapped her arms around herself and prayed a silent thank-you prayer. For the first time in nearly eighteen months, she realized she really did want to live after all.

That night she slept dreamlessly. Or if she had dreamed, she hadn't been disturbed by the content. She awoke feeling refreshed and renewed. But still she needed to decide what to do. Pack everything up and leave for good or plan on returning after the show? On one hand, it felt as if her work here was done. She'd made her painting breakthrough—as well as her emotional and even spiritual one too. Really, she was ready to go. Then why didn't she feel ready? With Christmas just around the corner, she knew the smart thing would be to go home. Why would she want to spend the holidays here, all alone—in such complete isolation?

She wondered what Anna and Garret would do during Christmas. Was there a wife and mother somewhere? If so, where? But why was she troubling herself with all these questions that had absolutely nothing to do with her?

"What do you think, Michael?" she asked as they walked outside. "You want to go for a really long ride today?"

His tail began to wag, and as crazy as it seemed, she let that be her sign—at the same time chiding herself for allowing the least necessary piece of canine anatomy to be the deciding factor of her fate. But it was better than flipping a coin. Still, by the time she got the cabin completely cleared out and the back of her Jeep packed, she felt unsure. And it bothered her that Anna would be expecting to hear from her again about caring for the dog.

Finally she decided to go back inside and write Anna a quick note that she could leave with Lucy (who also handled what little mail came to the local post office boxes). Apologizing for her change in plans, Claire wrote that she'd decided it was time for her to leave for good, and she had no choice but to take Michael along with her. She also encouraged Anna to continue pursuing her art dreams and thanked her and her father once again for rescuing her. Then she signed her name and sealed the envelope. She didn't bother to put a return address on it since it wasn't being mailed from the city, and there was little chance that Lucy wouldn't get it into the right box. Then she took one last look around the cabin, making sure everything was in its place, and much cleaner and nicer than when she'd first arrived. She locked the door and slipped the key back into the secret hiding place and, telling herself that she was doing the right thing, left.

But she felt a lump growing in her throat as she navigated the Jeep through the accumulation of snow—the roads had only been plowed once and that had been a couple weeks earlier. By the time she reached the store, she had recovered.

"Can you put this in the Henderson post office box?" she asked.

"Sure." Lucy examined the name on the front. "Oh, so you've met young Anna, have you? Isn't she the sweetest little thing?"

Claire nodded. "Yes. And she aspires to be an artist too."

"Well, isn't that perfect. Maybe you can give her some lessons—"

"Actually, I'm leaving now, Lucy."

"Leaving?" Lucy frowned. "You mean for good?"

"Yes. I think I've accomplished what I set out to do here."

Lucy leaned forward as if examining Claire. "And what was that, exactly?"

Claire smiled. "I needed to get back to my art. I'd been sort of blocked, if you know what I mean."

"Blocked? A good artist like you?" Lucy shook her head. "What in tarnation could block someone with your kind of talent?"

Claire had never divulged any of her history to this old woman before, but considering how Lucy had been such a good friend, not to mention working out the deal with her dog, she didn't mind telling her a bit more now. "Actually, I lost my husband and son about a year and a half ago and—"

"Oh, dear!" Lucy reached over and grabbed her hand in hers. "You don't have to explain another thing, honey. I know exactly what you mean. Why, when I lost my Walter, about ten years back, I was a perfect mess. Good grief, it took me several years to pull myself together. I let the store just go to wrack and ruin—Walter would've been furious with me." She laughed. "Maybe he was."

"But it looks like you're doing fine now."

"And so are you, honey. You're doing just fine. I can tell."

"Thanks for being a friend." Claire smiled. "I appreciate it."

"Well, you come back and visit now, ya hear?"

Claire waved as she opened the door. "I'll try to, Lucy. Maybe when the weather gets warm again."

The driving was much better on the main highway, with the pavement fairly clean and dry. They made a quick lunch stop and a couple of stops in between, but the closer Claire got to the city, the more excited she became.

"I've got a big show this weekend," she told Michael as she drove. "And you'll have to spend some time on your own for a while, over at Jeannie's, but you'll be okay, won't you?" She reached over and patted his head. "And I'll see about getting us into a bigger place, something with a yard for you to play in." She frowned. A yard? In the city? Who was she kidding? "Well, who knows, maybe we'll move out of the city." She smiled at the thought. "Actually, we can move wherever we want, Michael." She took in a deep breath, exhaling in a happy sigh. "Because I'm doing better. And I'm ready to move on." She almost regretted selling her big house now. But it had seemed too large and empty after losing Scott and Jeremy. And even with a dog she wouldn't need that much space now. No, it had been the right thing to do. She knew she'd find the perfect place eventually. She believed that God was directing her path from here on out.

On a hopeful hunch, she decided to give her landlord a call before she got to the city, just to see if there might be the slightest chance to get her lease changed to include a pet, even if it cost more. She explained the situation about adopting Michael in what she hoped was heart-warming detail, telling how he was an amazingly well-trained animal and how she would take all financial responsibility for everything and anything. And after a long pause he finally agreed to let her keep the dog, but only until Christmas.

"I'm sorry," he said, "but that's the best I can offer. And it's only because you've been a really good tenant. Unfortunately, I've had trouble with people and pets before. So I just can't allow more than a couple of weeks. However, if you're wanting to sublet your place, I do know of a woman who's looking for something just like it."

"Great, can you let her know I'm interested?"

"Sure."

She turned off her phone. "Well, Michael, we've got until Christmas to figure this out."

It was nearly midnight by the time she'd unloaded and put away everything from the Jeep. Michael had faithfully followed her up and down the three flights of stairs, and she hoped that maybe this would help to familiarize him with his new surroundings. She felt bad about uprooting this country dog to such an urban setting. But amazingly, he seemed to be fairly happy. Still, he didn't let her out of his sight.

"We'll lay low tomorrow," she promised him as she arranged an old army blanket for his bed right next to her own. She was glad that she'd returned a day before the opening; it would give them both more time to adjust. Being back in her old bed was a little unsettling. She recalled all the sleepless nights she'd spent tossing and turning there before. But perhaps it would be different now. Maybe this was the true litmus test as to whether she was really moving on or not.

To her surprise she slept fairly soundly again. Other than waking up a couple of times when she heard street noises below—a startling change after the silence of the cabin—she really did sleep well.

By midmorning, she was bored with puttering about her low-maintenance loft apartment, and she'd already taken Michael for a short romp in the nearby city park—a mere slip of land wedged between the packed-in housing. Finally she decided to set up her easel, ready to attempt an idea that had sprung up like a fertile seed, planted somewhere in the back of her mind. She'd been toying with it for a couple of days now. And it was time to see if she could really pull it off. It wasn't that she planned to put this in the show. But it was something she wanted to attempt.

By late that evening, she was finished. She washed out her brushes, and without looking at the painting, took Michael out for one last quick walk, then took a hot shower and collapsed exhausted into her bed.

The next morning, she got up just as the sun was rising. Feeling like a stranger in her own house, she tiptoed over to the easel and took a peek at yesterday's painting. With the morning sunlight gently diffused through a thin voile curtain, it was as if the painting was specially lit. She stared at the image with wide eyes, wondering if she'd really captured the likeness or whether her memory had simply transformed itself, meshing into her latest creation. But even if the portrait didn't look like Anna, it somehow captured the girl's spirit. And that's what she'd wanted. Oh, she knew the little girl wasn't really an angel. No doubt, she could probably be a little tyrant if she wanted to be. What child couldn't? But there was something in that face, her countenance, her innocence . . . something

Claire had been unable to forget ever since the day she'd met her.

Stepping back, she studied the picture more critically now. She wasn't sure why she'd painted a white bird in Anna's hands; she hadn't planned to in the beginning, but somehow it had just seemed to fit, with its feathery wings splayed open like a burst of living light. Really, this piece was beautiful. But then that was only *her* opinion. And she had been wrong before. She'd have to let Jeannie and Henri be the final judges.

She sighed, then shook her head. Why deceive herself? It was the public and the art critics who would be the final judges in this matter. And in all honesty it was the actual "patrons of the arts" who really determined whether any single work was a success or not. Because, despite what critics or contemporaries might think, it was that old bottom line that could make or break any show. She took in a deep breath and slowly exhaled, willing herself to calm. But the nagging fear wouldn't leave her. What if her show was a complete bust?

She filled her day with mundane chores, doing laundry, organizing a storage closet, walking the dog, paying bills. But by midafternoon she felt as if her nerves were all on edge. How would she manage to survive this opening? She fumbled to dial Jeannie's number, waiting impatiently until an assistant finally put her on the line.

"Jeannie?" she heard the urgency in her own voice.

"What's wrong, kiddo? You sound upset."

"I am! I mean, I'm totally freaked out." She took in a quick breath. "I just know they're going to hate me—my art. What *was* I thinking? *Angels?* Good grief! Why didn't you tell me that I was out of my mind? It's just way too sentimental, too weird. Oh, Jeannie—"

"Take it easy, Claire. It's going to be okay."

"I'll be a laughingstock. I'll probably never be taken seriously again. Is it too late to cancel the show? Can Henri get—"

"Relax, Claire. You're getting yourself all worked into a lather over nothing."

"Nothing?"

"Well, I'm not saying your art is nothing. But think about it—what is the worst that can happen? That's what my shrink always asks me. I mean, really, what's the worst case scenario here? That people won't like it? Won't get it? You won't sell anything?" Jeannie groaned. "Well, okay, even if that did happen, it wouldn't be the end of the world, would it?"

"I guess not."

"And I doubt that it would even end your career. People have pretty short memories when it comes to art. And besides, what if you hadn't painted those angels; where would you be right now?"

"Back at the cabin?" Suddenly Claire didn't think that sounded so bad—safe, secure, isolated.

"Yeah, and you'd be so down, you'd probably be ready to just give up."

"But if this show goes bust, I'll be ready—"

"I don't want to hear another word of negativity from you. You're killing my mood, and I need to be on my toes tonight. Now, let's change the subject. Tell me, when did you get into town anyway? And are you dropping Bowzer by my house?"

"We got here on Wednesday, and his name is Michael. I've got permission to keep him with me until Christmas."

"Great."

"But, Jeannie—"

"Only positive thoughts, Claire. I mean it."

"Right."

"Because just think about it, kiddo; it's like you're insulting whatever inspired you to paint those angels in the first place. Do you want to do that?"

Claire bit her lip. "No, not really."

"Okay then, this is what I want you to do. Go fill up that old claw-foot tub of yours with hot water and then add some really expensive bath salts—something soothing like lavender. Then put on a nice calming CD, light some candles, and just climb in and soak until the water cools off. After you're done, take a little nap, then get up and get dressed in something—uh, let me see—something heavenly. You got that?"

"I think so."

"And I'll come pick you up—"

"Oh, I can drive my—"

"No way. I'm not taking any chances. I'll be there around six—just to give us plenty of time."

12

Jeannie's prescription worked its magic on Claire, and by the time she got up from her nap, she felt a tiny glimmer of hope glowing within her. Maybe the evening wouldn't be so terrible after all. And if it was, she could always feign a headache and duck into the back room to lie down. She searched and searched her closet for something appropriate—was it "heavenly" that Jeannie had said? She'd be doing well to find something that fit, didn't need mending, and wasn't completely out of style. All the while she pulled out items, she berated herself for not having gone out and gotten something special for this evening. What had she been thinking? Finally, she came to a dress tucked way in the back of her closet. Something she'd almost forgotten. She pulled it out and gave it a shake. She barely remembered purchasing it. But as she recalled, it was supposed to have been for Scott's younger sister's wedding about three years ago. The couple, however, decided to elope, and as a consequence, the dress had never been worn. Claire wondered why she hadn't returned it then, but she'd liked it and probably hoped she could use it for something else.

The dress was a champagne-colored velvet—almost luminous, and perhaps slightly celestial or heavenly, if there were such a thing in earthbound apparel. It was the kind of fabric that seemed to just melt in your hand, soft and luxurious, flowing. That was probably why she'd kept it. It felt like liquid gold—only warmer. She held the dress before her in front of the mirror. The style, thankfully, was classic—as appropriate for today as it was three years ago.

Feeling a little like Cinderella, Claire slipped on the dress. But instead of a fairy godmother, she imagined that angels had prepared her finery for her. And why not? Her spirits buoyed even more when she found a pair of shoes that actually went with the dress. And her hopes for the evening continued to climb as she successfully pinned her hair into a fairly nice-looking chignon, slightly loose with a few strands curling around her bare neck. Then she inserted the antique pearl drop earrings that had been left to her by her mother. Perfect. She considered a rope of pearls around her neck, but that seemed a little too much. Just the earrings and her usual wedding ring would be sufficient jewelry for someone who'd worn little more than jeans and sweats for the last year and a half.

Standing before the mirror again, she admired her image with an artist's eye. The color of the dress was almost identical to her hair. Perhaps another reason she'd picked it.

She'd just finished adding a soft touch of makeup, the first she'd worn in ages, when the doorbell rang.

"Claire!" exclaimed Jeannie. "You look fabulous, dah-ling!" She laughed. "I'm serious, girl, you look stunning. Where'd you get that dress?"

"I found it in my closet."

"Shoot, I wish I could get so lucky." Jeannie tossed her cape onto the sofa and went to the refrigerator. "Mind if I get myself a soda?"

"Of course not. Let me get my coat and purse, and I'll be ready."

Claire had just located her coat when she heard Jeannie's scream. Running out of the bedroom, she nearly tripped over the dog. "What's wrong?" she cried.

"Oh, my word!" Jeannie was standing before the easel now. "This is absolutely gorgeous! When did you do it? And why isn't it in the show?"

Claire's hand was on her pounding chest. "Jeannie, you scared me to death! I thought you were being mugged or something."

Jeannie grabbed her arm. "I mean it, why isn't this in the show?"

"I don't know. I just did it. I wasn't even sure if—"

"Well, it's dry isn't it?" She gingerly tapped the edge. "Good. Grab some bubble wrap. We're taking it with us."

"But I'm not sure I want to sell it."

"Oh, Claire." Jeannie frowned at her, tapping the sharp point of her shoe on the hardwood floor.

"Really, Jeannie. I want to give it to someone."

Jeannie sighed. "Well, whatever. I suppose we can put a sold sign on it, but it *is* going in the show."

Claire practiced her deep breathing techniques as Jeannie drove them to Henri's gallery, praying silently that God would help her through this night. She wasn't asking for anything spectacular—mere survival would be sufficient.

"It's going to be okay," Jeannie assured her as she parked in back. "Leo's already written a rave review that came out in today's paper, but he'll be on hand just the same. And I've got a few other aces up my sleeve."

"Stacking the deck, are you?" Claire glanced uneasily at Jeannie as she carefully retrieved the painting from her trunk. "You afraid I might flop without some help?"

"No, I just like a little insurance; you could call it priming the pump."

Claire shook her head. "I think people can see right through your little devices, Jeannie. I mean, they're either going to like it or—" she controlled herself from using the word hate—"or they just won't."

"Claire! Claire!" Henri beamed as he met her at the door. He kissed her on both cheeks, then helped her to remove her coat and handed it to his assistant. "Oh, my!" He clasped his hands together. "You are such a vision—ah, the perfect companion to your lovely creations."

She looked right into his eyes. "So, really, Henri, be honest, do you like them?"

He pressed his lips together then nodded solemnly. "It is a very different type of show for me, but, yes, I do like them—very much so."

She knew that this was also his way of saying that he too felt unsure as to how the public might respond to her work. He, better than anyone, was well accustomed to the cynics and critics and snobs. And it was no secret that they could ruin an opening like this. For his sake, she hoped they wouldn't show at all—other than Leo that is.

Jeannie removed the bubble wrap from Claire's latest piece. *"Voila!"*

Henri clapped his hands. "Oh, it is exquisite. A prize! I know just where it will go." He turned around. "Andre! Come quickly." He whispered something to the man, then turned back to Jeannie and Claire. "Champagne?" he asked as a woman in a sleek black dress appeared with a tray. "And we have cheese and—" he waved his hands. "Oh, you know, it is the regular fare. Now if you will, please excuse me."

Claire leaned over to Jeannie. "He's nervous, isn't he?"

Jeannie nodded, taking a sip of champagne. "Let's give him a moment to place that last painting before we go in. You know how he likes the drama—to feel like the curtain's going up at the theater on opening night."

Claire swallowed. "I just hope it doesn't fall flat in the first act."

Jeannie scowled, then cautioned in a lowered voice, "No more negativity!"

"I'm sorry." Claire held up her hand. "I promise, no more."

Before long, Henri was ushering them into the gallery, waiting expectantly for their compliments and approval. And the truth was, Claire was impressed. His setup was flawless. The music was perfect. If the paintings flopped, the blame would be hers and hers alone.

"It's perfect, Henri," she said finally. "It couldn't be better. Thank you for taking such care." She looked around the carefully lit room. "Your gallery is really the best in the city, you know."

Jeannie held up her glass. "Best on the West Coast."

Claire laughed. "Best in the country."

Henri waved his hands as if to stop them. "Thank you, ladies. You make me blush."

People started to arrive now, slowly drifting through, quietly moving through the gallery in groups of twos and threes. Claire recognized a few of the faces and tried to be as friendly as seemed appropriate. She knew the early showing was for serious buyers, those who'd been specially invited—the type of people who would narrow their eyes and study a painting for several minutes, as if trying to see into the mind of the artist who painted it. Henri always served the best of the champagne first, and he scurried about, greeting his guests, introducing people, and commenting on various aspects of the art.

Claire could feel her hands trembling as she stood in a corner and watched their faces, unsure as to what they thought—one could never be sure. These were the kinds of people you would never want to play poker against. Their ability to conceal emotion was uncanny. And Claire knew it would be useless to try to read them tonight.

Like a puppet, she came when either Jeannie or Henri called, shaking the hand extended her way, smiling—but not too widely—aware that she could easily send the wrong message whether she meant to or not. She hated these shows—always had. But these were her dues, and in the art world, they had to be paid.

"Mrs. Campbell," she said. "It's such a pleasure to meet you. I've read of your work with the children's center—so wonderful."

"Thank you, dear." The woman pointed to one of Claire's earliest angel paintings. "And what inspired you to paint that?"

Claire swallowed. "It's hard to describe where inspiration comes from exactly . . ." she struggled for words. "I could say it's from some hidden place deep within me, and that wouldn't be untrue, but sometimes there seem to be other forces at work too." She smiled, but not too big.

"I see." Mrs. Campbell nodded as if she understood. Odd, since even Claire didn't completely understand herself. "Very nice, dear," said the older woman, as if talking to a preschooler about a finger painting.

Claire couldn't remember when the evening started to become fuzzy and hazy to her, and maybe it was the champagne, although she'd only had a few polite sips. But it was a blessing of sorts, like a form of protective insulation wrapping itself around her. And it helped to get her through all the varied and sometimes thoughtless comments that casual observers often make.

But finally, about midway through the show, and long after most of the serious art world had gone their way, to dinner reservations or some Christmas party or the comfort of their own homes, she slipped into the back room and sank into Henri's deep mohair sofa, leaning her head back with a loud sigh. She closed her eyes and tried to get everything she'd heard the last few hours to slide off her—like water off a duck's back, as her father would say. She'd talked him into coming on another night, when it wasn't so busy. But suddenly, she wished she'd begged him to make it tonight.

It would help to have someone else in her court right now. Someone unrelated and uninvolved in the precarious and unpredictable world of art. He could hold her hand and reassure her that it would be okay. No matter, if everyone here hated her work, if no one bought a single piece, if Henri quietly cancelled the remaining three weeks of the showing. Her father would put his arm around her and tell her that he loved her anyway. At least, that's the way she imagined it tonight. In reality, he might say something stupid like, "Maybe you should go back to teaching." He did that sometimes. Oh, she supposed it was only his practical side. But it always deflated her. Yes, perhaps it was better that he wasn't here to see her flop tonight.

"Claire?" Glenda, the woman in the sleek black dress, was standing in the doorway. "Someone here would like to meet you."

"Yes, of course." Claire stood and smoothed her dress. "I was just taking a break."

Glenda nodded without speaking. Claire wondered if she just thought she was being lazy, a slacker, like she didn't really care about the outcome of the showing. Claire followed this graceful woman in silence, wondering who could possibly be interested in the creator of these strange works that really wouldn't look good on anyone's wall.

And then she saw them. She blinked at first, thinking she must be imagining things. But there they were, Garret and Anna, both smiling at her as if she were a long-lost friend.

"What are you two doing here?" she exclaimed, taking each of them by a hand.

"We wanted to surprise you," said Anna.

Garret cleared his throat. "Actually, I'd promised Anna some Christmas shopping and—"

"I made him bring me here." Anna nodded victoriously.

"She didn't *make* me." Garret smiled. "I wanted to come."

"Claire, these paintings are—" Anna paused as if looking for the perfect word—"they're awesome."

"Thank you, Anna." Claire glanced around then spoke quietly. "That's the nicest thing anyone has said tonight."

Anna frowned. "You mean they don't like them?"

Claire shrugged then forced a smile. "It's hard to say."

"Then these people are all crazy."

"Anna." Garret spoke in a hushed but stern voice.

"Sorry." Anna looked up at Claire, then spoke in a quiet voice. "That one over there." She pointed toward the entrance. "Is *that*—?"

Claire grinned. "Yep. You recognize yourself?"

Garret was shaking his head in what seemed amazement. "But I don't get it, Claire. I mean how on earth did you manage—"

"I relied on memory." Claire guided them over to the painting of Anna. "I hope you don't mind."

"Of course not." Garret stared at the painting.

"I love it," said Anna. "And the bird is just perfect. I can't even explain why; it just is."

Claire sighed. "I hadn't planned on the bird at first, but he just came."

"But it's sold," said Anna, the disappointment plain in her voice.

Garret laughed. "We couldn't have afforded it anyway, sweetheart."

"Excuse me," interrupted Henri. "Can I borrow the artist from you, for just a moment, please?"

"Of course," said Garret. "We didn't mean to monopolize her."

The next instant, Claire was whisked off to meet the Fontaines, a wealthy couple who were seriously considering the painting that was set in the evening.

"I just love the dusky feel to it," said Mrs. Fontaine. "It reminds me of something. But I can't quite put my finger on it."

"Do you like Van Gogh?" asked Claire.

"That's it," said Mr. Fontaine. "It's like *Starry Night*."

Claire smiled. "Yes, that's what I thought when I finished it. I hadn't really meant it to be. Although I must admit to adoring Van Gogh. But when it was finished, I could see it too."

"Claire," called Jeannie.

Claire turned to see Jeannie motioning to her. "Will you excuse me, Mr. and Mrs. Fontaine," she said.

"Of course." Mrs. Fontaine smiled warmly. "It was so nice to meet you."

For the next ten minutes, Claire was shuffled around from customer to potential customer like a pinball. But the whole while she tried to keep a discreet eye on Garret and Anna, afraid they would soon grow bored and leave. She couldn't help but notice how handsome Garret looked with his hair combed and beard neatly trimmed.

Not that he hadn't looked handsome before. But tonight he looked more of a turn-your-head sort of handsome. Striking even. And she felt a slight flush climb into her cheeks as she accidentally caught his gaze upon occasion. She didn't really think it was just her imagination, but he almost seemed to be keeping an attentive eye on her too. Now, more than ever, she was thankful she'd taken the time to dress carefully. And yet she was troubled too.

As pleasurable as Anna and Garret's unexpected visit was, she still felt as if she'd been caught slightly off guard. And to experience such feelings of interest toward Garret was more than a little disturbing. She hadn't felt this way since—well, since Scott. And in a way, she felt as if she were betraying him now—just by *feeling* this way. She knew it was probably ridiculous and unfounded. After all, Garret was little more than a casual acquaintance. And even if he turned out to be something more, Scott, of all people, would surely want her to get on with her life. But still she felt unsure and slightly off balance. Finally, there came a lull in her introductions, and she knew it was time to return to Garret and Anna. She could tell by Garret's posture that he was moving toward the door. She knew it was time to say good-bye. And although it was something of a relief, it was a stinging disappointment as well.

"I'm sorry," she said as she rejoined them. "It got so busy all of a sudden."

"That's good, isn't it?" asked Anna.

"I don't know. But let's hope so." Claire glanced over her shoulder. "I'm so worried, mostly for Henri and Jeannie, that tonight's going to be a failure."

"But there are lots of people," said Anna hopefully.

"Yes, but so far, no sales." Claire sighed, then remembered Anna's portrait. "Other than the one, that is. And it's not for sure."

Garret nodded then spoke quietly. "And that's what pays the way, Anna. No matter how well we write or paint, we're always dependent on the folks who are willing to plunk down their money for our work."

He looked to Claire with what seemed compassion. "But it's easier for me, I think. The price of a book is a mere pittance compared to," he waved his hand, "all this."

Claire nodded. "I guess that's what makes me nervous."

Garret reached over and laid his hand on her shoulder. "Well, really, you shouldn't be." He looked her straight in the eyes, and for the second time she wondered about the actual colors she saw there—such a pleasant mix. "You are a great artist, Claire. And these paintings are bound to be a huge success. Just take a deep breath and relax. Let it all just come to you."

She felt almost as if he'd hypnotized her, and she just stood there for a full minute, just letting it soak in. Then she took a deep breath. "Thanks, Garret. I think I needed that."

"It's true," chimed in Anna. "You are a great artist."

Claire smiled—a big smile this time. "I'm so glad you two decided to drop in. I think I might actually be able to make it through the rest of the evening now."

"But is it true, you're not coming back to the cabin?" asked Garret.

"Yeah," said Anna. "We just barely got to know you—then poof, you're gone!"

Claire laughed. "Well, my work had been accomplished. Although I have to admit that I miss it already."

"Claire," called Jeannie again.

Claire nodded in her direction, then turned back to Garret. "I'm sorry—"

"No, we're the ones who should be sorry." He made another move toward the door. "We've been hogging all your time. Remember, you're the star tonight, Claire. Now, you get out there and shine."

She looked straight into his eyes for the briefest moment, mere seconds, although it felt like much more. Then she turned to Anna, afraid that actual tears now glistened in her own eyes, ready to betray feelings even she couldn't begin to fully understand. She gently squeezed Anna's hand, then glanced back to Garret. "Thank you, *both*, so much for coming."

"Our pleasure," said Garret.

"Bye, Claire," called Anna in a sweet voice as father and daughter exited together.

13

Claire knew she was quieter than usual during the ride home, but she had no words left—nothing she wanted to express, nothing she could say with any real meaning. Her mind felt jumbled—too many people, too many feelings. Overloaded. Yes, that was it. She felt like too many circuits had been operating at once and now she was drained, melting down.

"You okay, kiddo?" Jeannie glanced her way.

"Yeah, I guess."

"The show went pretty well, I think." Jeannie sighed. "Well, no big sales as yet, but sometimes it takes time. People need to go home and think about it, look at their walls, and the next thing you know a painting is speaking to them—they wake up the next morning certain they can't live without it."

Claire nodded. "Hope you're right."

"You sure you're okay?" Jeannie tapped her fingers on the steering wheel. "You seem a little depressed or something."

"Just overwhelmed, I think." Claire swallowed. "You know, after being alone—in the quiet—all those weeks, well, I . . ."

"Oh, I get it. Culture shock. Kind of like when the hermit comes back into society for the first time. Yeah, I bet tonight was a little taxing for you. Personally, I love these openings, but I must admit I feel a little frazzled afterwards. Still, I wouldn't give up this life for anything."

Jeannie continued to talk with enthusiasm, mentioning names of wealthy or important people—names that went right over Claire's head—people who might buy a painting or tell a friend or whatever. Claire wasn't really listening. She felt incapable of soaking in one more word, one more thought.

"Thanks for everything," she told Jeannie, climbing out of the car with weary relief. "Sorry I'm not much company."

Jeannie waved her hand. "Don't worry, kiddo. You did great tonight. That's what really matters. Now get some rest. Sleep in until noon tomorrow. Take it easy."

Claire nodded and closed the car door. As she slowly walked up the three flights of stairs, she remembered Michael. Hopefully, he'd been okay while she was gone. She hurried to unlock her door, suddenly worried that something might be wrong. But there he was, trotting happily toward her.

"Oh, you sweet thing!" she exclaimed, wrapping her arms around his neck. "How I missed you!"

Then she took him outside for a quick walk. The fog was thick tonight, not unusual for the Bay Area in December, but when she looked up at the streetlight now shrouded in heavy mist, she found herself missing the star-studded sky in the mountains—and the snow. She also found herself wondering where Garret and Anna were staying tonight. In the city? Or perhaps they had family or friends in a nearby suburb? Or did Garret have a house himself? She'd never thought to ask where they lived when not staying in the cabin. And once again she wondered if there was a wife, a mother, somewhere nearby. She turned and began walking quickly back to her apartment, irritated at herself for wondering on these things. What difference was it to her anyway? Garret and Anna *were* nice people, yes, and they had helped her in a time of dire need. But the relationship would surely go no further than this. Why on earth should it?

Back in the apartment, Claire realized she was pacing again. She went over to the bookshelf, which was still only half filled; boxes of books and various memorabilia were stacked nearby. She picked up a framed photo, just a candid shot that she'd managed to catch at Jeremy's soccer game, not long before the boating accident. Father and son were both smiling as they celebrated the win with a victory hug. Jeremy's hair curled around his forehead, damp with sweat, and his eyes shone, big and brown—the mirror image of his dad nearly twenty years earlier, or so his paternal grandma liked to brag. And Claire had no reason to doubt her. What a pair they were! And, as usual, she felt that old familiar pain in her chest when she gazed at the photo, only now it felt slightly different. As if the knifelike sharpness had left her or become dulled somehow, what with the passing of time and emotions poured out along the way. She knew it was right, and yet it felt totally wrong. Like a betrayal even. As if she had sneaked something behind their backs, or thrown away what was valuable, or simply run away.

"But you're the ones who are gone," she said aloud. "And you were the ones so bound and determined to go deep-sea fishing that day, even after I told you the forecast didn't look good. You were the ones with all the confidence and bravado, ready to take on the weather and bring home your trophy fish to hang on the wall above the fireplace." She set the photo down and sighed. She no longer felt angry at them, the way she used to during those rare moments when she allowed herself to remember that day and the way they so easily brushed off her warning.

She walked over to the window, the one that offered a view of the bay, on a clear day that is. Not tonight though. "I forgive you," she whispered into the glass that reflected her own image, although it was them she was seeing. "And I realize it's not your fault." She felt her eyes filling, but not with tears of rage this time. "You never intended to go out there and die. And you never meant to leave me all alone like this. It's just the way life happened." She took in a deep breath. "And I release you both now. I release you to celebrate eternity—to fly with the angels!" She smiled, tears slipping down her cheeks as she imagined the two of them flying with the angels, just like she'd done in her dream. And in that same moment, it was as if a heavy coat of iron mail began sliding off her shoulders. And she lifted her arms like wings, and leaning her head back, with fingers splayed, she took in a slow deep breath, then exhaled. And it tasted just like mercy!

14

"Henri would love for you to make another appearance," said Jeannie. "If you can manage it, that is. The weekend traffic was pretty good, and the 'starry night' painting sold, and we've had several promising bites on others too."

"That's great," said Claire. Cradling the phone between her head and shoulder, she returned to her work in progress and picked up a brush.

"I know you're not that crazy about public appearances, but Henri really thinks it would help to keep this ball rolling."

"Yeah, I'm not much into that whole meet the artist sort of thing, but I'm willing to do my part"—she daubed a little more blue in a corner—"if you really think it'll help the showing."

"Oh, you're a darling. How about both Thursday and Friday nights? That's when most of the traffic comes anyway, plus it'll still give me time to run another ad in Wednesday's paper."

"Sure." Claire twirled the paintbrush between her fingers. "And I might even have another painting for you."

"You're kidding! Oh, I can't wait. What's it like? Can you tell me?"

Claire studied the nearly completed work. "Well, as you can guess, it's angels again. But this time it's more of a seascape, more blues than whites; it's hard to describe really."

"Oh, it sounds wonderful. Let me know when to have it picked up."

"And Jeannie," Claire considered her words. "I think it might be my last."

"Your last?" Jeannie gasped. "What? What are you saying? You're not—I mean, I know you were depressed—"

Claire laughed. "I don't mean my last painting—ever! I mean my last *angel* painting. I just have this feeling that I've reached the end of my angel era. I'm ready to move on now."

"Oh." The relief was audible. "Well, that's okay, kiddo. To be honest, I'm not even sure how big this angel market really is, but, hey, we're giving it our best shot. And so far, we're not disappointed."

"Good. I think you can probably send someone by to pick this one up by Wednesday."

The week progressed slowly for Claire. She found herself missing the snow and the mountains and, to be perfectly honest, Garret and Anna. Although she kept telling herself this was completely ridiculous. Good grief, she barely knew them. Had only experienced two very brief and somewhat unusual encounters with them. But still, she missed them and wished for the chance to know them better. Not only that, she felt fairly certain that Michael was homesick too. He seemed to be lagging lately, and his tail didn't wag nearly so often or so vigorously as before. The city was a poor place to keep a dog like him. She wondered if he might not even be happier in his old, albeit slightly neglectful home, penned up with the other dogs.

She stooped and stroked his head on her way out the door. It was her last night to make an appearance at the showing. "I'm sorry, boy, I have to go out again tonight. But I promise to take you for a nice long walk tomorrow. We'll go to the park and chase sticks or something."

She tried not to notice the lights and decorations for Christmas as she drove through the city. And, although it wasn't nearly as bad as the previous year had been—her first Christmas without them—she still felt lonely. Her father had invited her down to Palm Springs again, to join him and some of his retired friends for the holidays, and she'd told him she'd think about it, but somehow she just didn't think that was where she wanted to be this year. Not that she knew exactly.

Once again, Claire followed Jeannie and Henri around the gallery—the congenial marionette, jumping whenever they pulled the strings. She greeted potential customers, all the while smiling and conversing, trying to appear relaxed and comfortable when she was anything but. Still, there did seem to be a good-sized crowd moving in and about—even better than the week of the opening.

"Word's gotten around," whispered Jeannie as the evening began drawing to a close with only a few stragglers remaining behind, picking at what remained of the cheese and crackers and finishing off a bottle of cheap champagne. "To think we had this much business tonight, and just a week before Christmas—not bad."

"And Leo's review didn't hurt any either," said Claire. "Remind me to send him chocolates or something."

Jeannie laughed. "Don't worry, I already did. And you've had a couple other good reviews too."

Claire felt her eyebrows lift. "And no bad ones?"

Jeannie shrugged. "Hey, you can't please all the people all the time."

"I figured as much." Claire smiled. "That's why I still think ignorance is bliss when it comes to reviews."

Jeannie patted her arm in a placating way. "For some people perhaps."

After the gallery closed, Jeannie invited Claire to go across the street for a cup of cappuccino with her. "Unless you're totally exhausted, that is. As for me, I always need several hours to unwind before I can even think about sleep."

"Sure, that sounds good. As long as it's decaf."

"Well, Henri seems very pleased," said Jeannie after a pair of large mugs were placed on the table. "He sold another painting tonight and expects to sell another to the Van Horns tomorrow."

"Which ones?"

"Tonight was the foggy one. I'm not sure which one the Van Horns are interested in."

Claire smiled. "That is so cool—three paintings sold within a week! I hope the paintings last as long as the show."

Jeannie laughed. "Now, wouldn't that be something? Oh, by the way, someone inquired about consignments the other day. Do you want to consider it?"

Claire frowned. "I don't know if I could. I mean not with the angels anyway. It's not your everyday kind of painting, you know? It's like an idea just hits me, all at once like an inspiration, and I pour it out onto canvas—almost without thinking, although I know that doesn't make sense. I don't think I could have someone actually directing me in this."

Jeannie waved her hand. "No problem. I sort of hinted at that to the woman. Besides, she seemed pretty interested in your latest one anyway, the seascape."

Claire took a sip of coffee. She hadn't really wanted to sell that one, but after already hanging onto two of them, she felt she'd better let it go. Especially since that's what the picture had been about anyway—*letting go.*

"I've also had several people ask about the one with the bird in her hands. It's a shame you don't want to sell that one." Jeannie drummed her long painted fingernails against her coffee cup, making a ringing sound, almost like bells. "But you know, Claire, perhaps that's one we should consider having some numbered and signed prints made from, that and a couple of the others. Had you thought about that?"

"No, but it sounds like a good idea. If you really think they'd sell."

"I'll look into it first thing in the morning. I don't know why I didn't think of it sooner."

Claire had to laugh. "You are such a businesswoman."

"Good thing one of us is." Jeannie studied her carefully. "You seem to be doing better, Claire. Or is it just wishful thinking on my part?"

Claire briefly told her about her recent letting go episode and how she felt more at peace than ever before. "It was such a simple thing to do really. I don't know why it took me so long."

"Just a matter of timing, I suspect. You can't force some things."

"But I have been thinking about something . . ."

Jeannie's eyes lit up. "What? A new project? Tell me."

Claire smiled. "No, not a new project. Actually, I was considering going back to the cabin—I mean if it's okay with you—"

"You're kidding! You want to go back up there again?"

She nodded. "I know it probably sounds crazy, especially this time of year—"

"You're serious? You want to go up there now? Right in the middle of winter and just days before Christmas? Are you *really* all right, honey?"

Claire felt her cheeks grow warm. "Okay, Jeannie, I'll tell you something, but it's just between you and me, okay? Because I could be all wet and about to make a total fool of myself."

Jeannie leaned forward. "I'm in! Quick, tell me everything before I keel over from curiosity."

"Okay, do you by any chance remember a man and his daughter—they came in on opening night last week, and I spent some time talking to them?"

Jeannie's brows shot up. "Yes! A very handsome man—sort of a Robert Redford type, only I think this guy had a beard, didn't he? Now, I don't normally care for full beards like that, but as I recall it looked good on him. And a pretty little girl—" she snapped her fingers. "A girl who looked strikingly like a certain angel I've seen somewhere. Tell me more!"

Claire giggled. "Remember the Hendersons up in the mountains—the people you told me about?"

"The ones with the cabin not too far from ours?"

"Yes. Well, have you ever heard of an author—a G. A. Henderson?"

"Historical novels?"

Claire nodded. "The Hendersons' son. I met him and his daughter up there."

"Aha, now it's all starting to make sense. Do I smell romance in the air?"

"No, no. Not romance. But I did find them both, well, interesting. And I want to get to know them better. I mean, I hardly even know them at all, but . . ."

"Sometimes you know certain things . . . almost instantly . . ." Jeannie's eyes grew slightly dreamy. "It's like—you know, one of those things . . . you can just tell when you first meet someone that there's something more." She shook her head and chuckled. "Unfortunately it takes some of us years before we really figure it out."

Claire studied Jeannie. "You mean you've got something romantic going?"

Jeannie smiled coyly.

Suddenly Claire knew. "It's Leo, isn't it?"

"Now, don't you say a word to anyone. I'm not even totally sure myself yet."

"That is so perfect."

"Well." Jeannie set down her cup. "That settles it then."

"What?"

"You've *got* to go back to the cabin."

"I don't know. I mean, I was only considering it; I'm not really positive it's such a good—"

"No arguing. Now, when are you leaving?" She looked at her watch. "Good grief, I should let you get on your way right now; that way you can start packing tonight. You can leave first thing in the morning and be up there just past noon."

"But—"

"No buts. You better get going, kiddo. Look at it this way. It's still, what, three days until Christmas? And if you find out you're wrong about this guy, say in the next day or so, well, you can just cut your losses and hop in your car and get back to whatever it is you were planning to do for Christmas."

"I didn't really have any plans—"

"Well, then you'll just have to join Leo and me and some of our other single friends."

"But what if he's not there, or what if he's—"

"I said *no buts.*" Jeannie picked up her purse and started to stand. "Now, it's time for you to be on your way, kiddo. No argument. And don't worry, the showing will get along just fine without you for the next week. Just promise to keep me posted on this." She clapped her hands. "Oh, this is just too good! I can't wait to write the press release—something like 'famous writer and artist soon to be wed'! How about on Valentine's Day? This is fantastic!"

"Oh, Jeannie." Claire shook her head in mock disgust. "You are such an opportunist!"

Jeannie frowned. "I thought you were going to say a romantic."

Claire laughed. "Well, how about if we make a deal? I'll pursue my romantic dream—as crazy as it seems—if you'll pursue yours, which happens to be practically sitting in your lap."

Jeannie stuck out her hand. "Deal?"

"Deal." And they shook on it.

15

Without allowing herself the luxury of even considering what it was she was about to leap into, Claire followed Jeannie's instructions to a T. She went straight home, began packing her things, and was ready to leave the following morning. But instead of leaving first thing in the morning, she waited around long enough for the gallery to open, then called Henri.

"I hate to bother you, Henri, and please feel free to say no, but you know the angel picture—the one with the girl holding the bird?"

"Yes. The one I am not allowed to sell?"

"Right. I wonder if you would mind if I took that one with me today. It's meant to be a Christmas gift—"

"Of course. You come and get it whenever you like. It might help some of the other paintings to sell, you know, taking away that unavailable distraction."

"Yes." She considered this. "I can see what you mean."

So, before leaving town, she swung by the gallery and picked up the painting, then tucked it safely into the backseat of her Jeep. Even if Jeannie decided it was worth reproducing copies from, they could always borrow it back later for scanning.

"Well, here we go, Michael." She smiled at him as she pulled back into the traffic. "I hope this isn't a great big mistake."

But Michael's tail thumped happily, as if he knew that it wasn't a mistake at all, and as if he knew he was going home. While she drove, she kept a constant train of CDs going, all her old favorites, trying to fill the space and to keep herself from thinking about what she was actually doing. She was afraid if she really considered all things carefully and the limited chances of success, she would simply turn back and forget the whole thing. And she really didn't want to turn back.

It was afternoon by the time she reached the cabin. Michael was so happy that he leaped from the car and ran around in circles, barking wildly and rolling in the snow. She immediately went inside and started a fire. She knew the cabin would feel like an ice chest after sitting vacant for more than a week. Then, taking her time, she unloaded her things. She had already decided not to visit Garret and Anna today. She needed some time to settle in, to prepare herself and gather up her nerve. But she could take Michael for a nice long walk—she had promised him as much yesterday. Of course, she had expected it to be within the city limits at the time. Now, the space was limitless, or so it seemed.

With the fire stoked up and burning brightly, she bundled up in preparation for their walk. She tried not to remember their last walk—the time when they'd become lost and nearly frozen in the woods. But then it had turned out all right, all things considered. For how else would she have met them? Fortunately, there was no threat of snow today. The sky was perfectly clear and bluer than a robin's egg, and the snow shone clean and bright, recently dusted with a fresh coat of powder.

"All right, Michael," she said as she opened the door. "Let's go!"

Everything was the same as she remembered—only better. Much, much better! The trees seemed taller and greener, and the smell—why, the smell was almost intoxicating. Why hadn't she noticed that before? Air so clean and fresh, a person might become rich if they could somehow bottle it up and sell it as a health tonic in the city. She paused to notice the various tracks crisscrossing through the snow, the usual rabbits and squirrel and deer and birds. Oh, what a story something as simple as snow could tell! She continued on until she came to the dead tree, then stopped just to admire its flawless form once again dusted with glistening snow. Of course, she realized—she must paint it! She walked around, considering it from various angles, finally deciding on the way she always found it on her walks, pointing to the right, as if indicating which way the trail went. She was glad she'd brought her camera to the cabin this time. She'd have to remember to carry it with her on all her walks. Who knew what other great things she might discover out here, things full of inspiration and worthy of painting—

Suddenly she stopped. Frozen in her tracks, she stared down at the trail before her. Her hand flew to her mouth, but in the same instant she told herself not to worry, that it was nothing really. Nothing that should concern her anyway. Not really. Still she stayed put. Michael paused up ahead, turning to look back at her, his head cocked to one side as if to inquire about why she'd stopped.

"It's okay, boy," she finally assured him, forcing herself to continue walking forward and averting her eyes from what it was that had so stunned her.

Three sets of footprints. There were three sets of footprints today. Two pairs looked familiar. She easily recognized them as Garret and Anna's—the same she had seen so many times before. But the third set, the new ones, looked to be a woman's boots—about the same size as her own. She knew this for certain on first glance. And in her mind's eye she could see the three of them walking together too. The happy family—husband and wife and child.

Well, of course, she chided herself, why wouldn't he have a wife? And why shouldn't sweet Anna have a mother? It was only normal. What had made her think otherwise? Certainly nothing he'd said, and nothing from Anna had misled her in this regard. It had simply been her own stupid assumption. The wife probably worked, maybe in the city. Perhaps she kept things together in their home while Garret went off to write in the woods. And why not? She knew plenty of people who lived somewhat independent lives—especially creative people. Oh, why hadn't she seriously considered this possibility before? She brushed away a cold tear that had streaked down her cheek, and fighting against the lump in her throat, told herself to be an adult. "Get over it!" she said in a sharp voice, causing Michael to turn and look curiously at her.

"Not you, Michael," she said in a friendly but forced tone. "You're a good ol' boy." Happy with this praise, he continued along, and obediently she followed him, moving her feet like a pair of leaden boots and wishing she were at the bridge so she could finish her walk, turn back, and go home—back to San Francisco.

She blew out a long puff of air, watching it turn into white steam as it hit the frigid air, then quickly vanished. And what difference did it make that he was married anyway? What was it to her? It certainly didn't change anything. Garret and Anna had still been good friends to her. Good grief, they had literally saved her life. So why on earth should she think of them any differently now? It was silly for her to react like this. Childish even. And, she told herself sternly, she would still give Anna that portrait—partly as a thank-you and partly as a Christmas present. A very valuable present, of course, but then Anna was special. And for some reason Claire felt she deserved the portrait. Sure, it wouldn't be easy to take it up to their door and perhaps risk meeting the mother—the wife— but then, it would be necessary. And maybe it was a good way for her to simply close this door and move on.

Claire paused at the bridge, taking a moment to touch it, then turned around and began walking quickly back, averting her eyes from the trail in front of her. But as she walked, she prayed. She confessed to God that she felt disappointed and sad by this new revelation. But she also asked him to help her move through it.

"You've gotten me through so much more than this," she said aloud as she walked. "I know you can help me with this too. I trust you."

It was just getting dusky when they reached the cabin, and despite her longing to get out of that place, to return to the city and to never, never look back, she realized the wisdom in waiting until morning before she made her final exodus. Besides, she needed to drop off the painting for Anna. She briefly considered calling Jeannie and telling her the disappointing news, but what if Jeannie used this as an excuse not to pursue her chances with Leo? Claire would wait until she returned to the city—or maybe even after the holidays. Why should she crash their happy Christmas gathering and be forced to share her pathetic story? Then, realizing that Jeannie might actually call her, she unplugged and turned off her cell phone. She had no desire to hear Jeannie's voice oozing with sympathy. That would only serve to unleash the sadness inside her—the sadness that she had, so far, managed to keep mostly at bay.

She went to bed early that night, worried that this most recent distress might disturb her sleep with restlessness or troubling dreams, but when she awoke the next morning, she felt surprisingly rested and peaceful. While she went about her chores of cleaning and repacking, and finally reloading the Jeep, she could almost feel Michael's confusion; he studied her with quiet canine curiosity—as if he somehow knew she was making a huge mistake. Perhaps he wanted to ask her if she really intended to take him back to the confines of that city, but being a dog, he simply remained silent but watchful.

She knew she had one more thing to do, and it would take everything in her to do it. She backed out the Jeep and pointed it in the direction of the Henderson cabin, and with unexplainable resolve willed herself to drive there. It took only a few minutes by road—unlike the snowy day when she'd followed their tracks through the woods. It was only as she pulled up that she noticed a different vehicle in the driveway—not the SUV Garret had driven her home in that day. This was a sensible, dark green Subaru—one of those wagon-types with all-wheel drive—very safe and good in snow. A family car, probably his wife's.

After parking her Jeep and practicing her smile—the same one that came in so handy during art showings—she opened the back door to retrieve the painting. It was too late to turn back now. She reminded herself of one of her dad's favorite sayings—what doesn't kill you will make you stronger. But even so, she fought back feelings of dread and foolishness as she tramped through the snow and onto the porch. Gritting her teeth, she knocked resolutely on the door, hoping against hope that Anna would be the one to open it.

"Hello?" said a pretty, dark-haired woman, thirty-something, petite, and wearing an oversized charcoal gray sweater—probably one of Garret's.

"Hello." Claire smiled, but not too big. "I'm sorry to intrude like this, but this is for Anna—"

"Oh, my goodness!" The woman stared at the painting. "Why that's absolutely beautiful!" She looked back at Claire, astonishment written all over her face. "Oh, excuse my terrible manners; I'm Louise; I'm—"

"Can you give it to her, please?"

"But won't you come inside and—"

"No." Claire firmly shook her head. "I mean, I would, but my dog's in the car, and we've got to be on our way; we're going back to San Francisco and—"

"But Anna's not here right now. They went sledding just a bit ago—Garret had been promising her and—"

"Oh, that's okay." Claire waved her hand. "Just tell them Merry Christmas for me and—"

"But, please, can't you come in and just visit for a few minutes?"

In desperation, Claire shoved the portrait toward this disturbingly friendly woman. Why couldn't she have been someone a little less likable? Claire felt her chin trembling now, a sure sign that she was about to lose it. "No," she said firmly. "No, I can't. I'm sorry, but I've really got to get going now."

Louise took the painting and shook her head. "This is such a wonderful present. I just wish you could stay a bit and—"

"Sorry." Claire turned and hurried back to her car, not even pausing to look as the woman called out to thank her and say good-bye.

Claire started her engine, pretending to intently study her rearview mirror as she backed out of the driveway, but mostly she was trying to see past the blurry curtain that was slipping over her eyes.

"Just relax," she said aloud as she drove back down the road and eventually past her cabin—rather, Jeannie's cabin. She took in several deep, calming breaths, then continued driving deliberately on—not too fast and not too slow. That really hadn't gone so badly, all things considered. She hadn't made a complete fool of herself. And Louise really did seem like a nice person—good mother and wife material. That was something, really it was. And before long, this would all be just a distant memory—perhaps she and Jeannie would even laugh about it, in time. "Remember the time I dared you, and you took off over the mountains hoping to find your true love," Jeannie would chortle, "only to discover that the poor man was already happily married?" And then they would throw back their heads and laugh.

But not today. There would be no laughing today. She slipped a CD into the player, careful to pick an upbeat one, turning the volume up just slightly. Then she reached over and patted Michael's head. "Hey, I still have you, boy." She tried to make her voice sound light and cheerful. Then more apologetically, "But I'm sorry you have to go back to the city now. I didn't mean for this to be such a quick trip. We'll figure out something better than that old apartment for you. I promise, we'll find something that has room for you to run around. It won't be so bad, really, it won't."

16

Before heading onto the highway, Claire decided to stop by the little store. It would be her last chance to say good-bye to Lucy and get a cup of coffee. Not the best coffee, to be sure, since Lucy was of the old school and believed the best coffee came from a great big red can labeled "mountain grown." No freshly ground Starbucks would ever be found in her little store, no-sir-ee, not as long as she still ruled behind the counter.

Claire parked her Jeep in the deserted parking area in front of the little store. Christmas Eve was obviously not Lucy's busiest time. In fact, Claire had wondered if she'd even be open today. "Want to get out and stretch your legs once more before we hit the road?" she asked Michael, holding the passenger door open while he jumped down. "I'll just be a minute."

Claire tried to smile as she opened the door, tried to appreciate the irony of the cheesy artificial wreath—a sharp contrast to the real, live evergreens growing in abundance all about the place. "Merry Christmas!" she called when she spied Lucy stooped over a cardboard carton in the rear of the store.

"Is that you, Claire?" Lucy stood up slowly, rubbing her back. "What on earth are you doing up here the day before Christmas?"

Claire considered her answer. "Well, I just had an errand that brought me this way again."

Lucy frowned. "So, you're just passing through then?"

Claire nodded. "Yep. But I thought I should stop by to say hello before I head back to the city. And I'll take a cup of your coffee for the road."

"You got some big plans for the holidays?" Lucy reached for the stained coffee carafe and started to fill a large-sized Styrofoam cup with what looked like very black and thicker than usual coffee.

"I'll probably just be with friends."

Lucy held out the cup. "This one's on the house, Claire. Merry Christmas."

"Thanks. How about you, Lucy? Do you have any plans for Christmas?"

The old woman laughed. "Ha. Not hardly. I'll probably just take home some old movies and park my tired body in front of the television."

Knowing that Lucy was a widow, Claire wondered if she had any family nearby but knew better than to ask, especially considering Lucy's obvious lackluster plans for the holidays. No sense in forcing the old woman to explain what could very well be painful to talk about. Besides, Claire knew as well as anyone how it felt to answer those kinds of questions. Who liked to admit they would be alone for the holidays? It sounded so pathetic. Besides that, such pitiful admissions only served to make the asking party feel bad, guilty even, as though it were somehow their fault that they hadn't been as unfortunate.

"Well, I better be on my way now. Thanks for the coffee, Lucy."

"You drive careful. And come see me again—next time you're in this neck of the woods, that is."

Claire went back outside, expecting to find Michael sitting patiently on the porch, just like he always did when she came to the store. But he didn't seem to be around. "Michael?" she called. She went over to the Jeep, thinking he could be waiting over there, but still no sign of the dog. Now she whistled, expecting him to shoot around the corner, but still he didn't come. Worried, she set her coffee cup on the hood of her car and began to look around, calling his name. Where could he have gone? It wasn't like him to take off like this.

She heard the bell tinkle on the door and turned to see Lucy peering out at her. "Something wrong?" called the old woman.

"It's my dog," explained Claire. "He seems to have taken off."

"He didn't head to the highway, did he?" Lucy looked toward the main road where a big semi was streaking by, its chained tires clinking in rhythm to the wheels.

Claire felt a jolt of fear run through her at the thought of Michael venturing onto the highway. "Oh, surely he wouldn't."

Then Lucy nodded toward a stand of pines behind the store. "Hey, there's some tracks going that way."

"Yes!" Claire followed them with her eyes. "And they look like dog tracks. I'll go see if that isn't him. But if you see him around, could you keep him on the porch until I get back?"

"You bet."

Claire hurriedly followed the tracks into the trees, not completely sure they belonged to Michael, but not convinced they didn't either. She continued calling his name and whistling. But the tracks just seemed to go deeper and deeper into the woods, and the more she looked at them, the more she wondered if they actually belonged to her dog at all. Finally, she bent down and felt of a paw print, but the impacted snow had a crusty edge to it, as if this trail was from the previous day. She turned around and began to jog back to the store, fearing the worst—why hadn't she gone up to check the highway first? Maybe he was trying to go back home. She felt tears sting her eyes as she started to run. What if he'd been hit? Oh, how could she possibly endure another loss right now? How much could one person take? With each step she prayed, silently begging God to spare her dog. It didn't seem too much to ask. This morning had been hard, but to possibly lose Michael too—that would surely push her over the edge.

She emerged from the woods to spot another vehicle now parked in front of the store. A dark blue Ford Explorer—and it looked a lot like the one Garret drove.

And, yes, to complicate matters further, there stood Garret and Anna along with a couple of other people she had never seen before.

"Claire!" cried Anna, waving wildly. "We've got your dog here."

Claire sighed in relief and hurried toward them. Perhaps seeing them wouldn't be so bad after all, as long as Michael was okay.

"Lucy said you'd lost him," said Anna, as she and the dog ran over to join Claire. Michael looked perfectly fine, if not somewhat pleased with himself as his tail wagged happily behind him.

"What got into you, boy?" Claire asked as she knelt down and stroked the dog's head. "You had me really worried."

"We saw him walking by the road," explained Anna breathlessly. "I told Dad that I knew it was your dog, but he didn't believe me at first. Then I made him stop, and we picked up Michael and brought him over here. And then we saw Lucy, and she told us that you'd lost him."

"Thank you," said Claire, standing. "Once again, you came to my rescue." She tried to keep her eyes from glancing over to where she knew Garret was standing.

"Claire!" he called out, waving.

She looked his way and waved weakly. She longed for a quick and easy escape, some way to avoid what promised to hurt, but knew she must do the mature thing. "Hi, Garret," she called, mustering a bravado she didn't feel. "Thanks for picking up my dog. I really don't know what got into him."

He was walking toward her now, a big smile on his face. "Anna's the one who first saw him. And even then I thought it was simply hopeful imagining on her part." He laughed. "But she was right. And here you are."

"See, Dad!" She poked him in the arm. "I *knew* it was Michael."

"What are you doing here?" he asked, his eyes peering into hers with an intensity that threatened to undo her.

She felt a tightness in her chest as she averted her eyes and pretended to adjust her leather gloves. "I—I needed to take care of something—at the cabin." Then she remembered the portrait. "And, well, I had something to leave for Anna—"

"For *me?*" Anna's eyes lit up. "What? What is it?"

"Actually, I already dropped it by your cabin." Claire fumbled in her coat pocket for sunglasses, a good cover-up, just in case.

"Then you met Louise?" he asked.

"Yes." She slipped on the dark glasses and returned his gaze now. He was still smiling, that same slightly crooked smile, and his eyes shone mostly blue in the bright sunlight, or maybe they were simply reflecting the blue of his parka.

"So, how long are you staying?" he asked.

"Oh, I'm on my way home."

"Already?" Anna's disappointment was plain in her voice.

"Yes, it's Christmas Eve, you know." Claire pressed her lips together. "I really should be going now."

"I'm sorry," said Garret, as he noticed the man and little boy now coming over to join them. "I guess I should've introduced you to my brother-in-law Doug and my nephew Hayden. We were all out sledding this morning."

"You must be the famous artist." Doug grinned as he shook her hand. "Anna's been going on and on about you. And my wife's been literally praying to meet you."

"Well, her prayers have been answered," said Garret. "Claire dropped something by the cabin just this morning."

"You're kidding! Man, I'll bet she was totally beside herself when you showed up!" Doug slapped her on the back. "Wow, I'm surprised she actually let you get away so easily."

Claire narrowed her eyes, studying him closely, unsure as to whether she'd heard him correctly or not. "You mean *Louise?* Louise is your wife?"

"Yeah, we came up here to spend Christmas with the family." He pretended to punch Garret. "We'd heard this guy was turning into a hermit, so we all decided it was time to come on up to the mountains and stir him up a little. The folks are coming too."

Anna grabbed Claire's arm, whispering urgently, "Please, can you tell me what it is?"

"What?" asked Claire, feeling slightly dizzy. She suddenly felt the need to sit down and put her head between her knees, or perhaps drink a cool glass of water or just breathe or something.

"What it is that you brought me," explained Anna, her eyes wide with anticipation.

"Oh." Claire remembered the painting. "But it's for Christmas. It should be a surprise."

"But can't you come back to the cabin for a little while?" begged Anna, gently tugging on her arm. "Aunt Louise is making chicken enchiladas for lunch."

Claire looked helplessly toward Garret, then over to her Jeep—her escape from all this. Of course, she *was* relieved to learn that Louise wasn't his wife, but did that really change anything? *Really?* Her strong reaction to meeting Louise this morning had both shocked and frightened her—she'd been unaware that she cared that much. And even now, she had no guarantees that there wasn't a wife—hiding away somewhere—ready to pop out at any given moment. And even if there were no wife, why on earth should she stick around and risk more pain? "I . . . I really should go," she said weakly.

"But it'll be lunchtime soon," urged Anna, sounding more mature now. "And you'll have to stop to eat anyway, won't you? Why not just stay a little longer and eat lunch with us?"

"We'd love to have you," added Garret. "And Louise is a really great cook."

"Yeah!" agreed Anna with youthful enthusiasm. "She's the one who taught me everything I know, which is pretty important since Dad's totally hopeless in the kitchen."

"I know Louise would be thrilled to have you," said Doug. He looked down to see his small son now hopping from one foot to the other. "Excuse me, but I think Hayden may need to visit the little boys' room."

"Please, come!" Anna peered up at Claire hopefully.

Claire looked at Garret and, despite herself, thought he looked hopeful too. "Well, I suppose I—"

"Yes!" Anna made a victory fist.

"Great," said Garret. "Why don't you go on ahead of us. We need to pick up a few things at the store, and then we'll meet you at the cabin."

Claire walked over to her Jeep, feeling almost as if she were in a dream. But as she opened the door for Michael, she realized what she'd just agreed to. What had she been thinking? What was the sense of putting herself into what seemed a very precarious position when she obviously lacked the emotional stamina to survive more pain? Why hadn't she simply made her excuses and run? But how could she back out now? She drove back toward the cabin, feeling dazed. But as she drove, she prayed. And as she prayed, she felt a faint glimmer of hope—like maybe she could get through this after all.

"You're back?" said Louise as she threw open the door. "Oh, I'm so glad. Can you come in?"

Claire nodded dumbly as she was led inside. "I—uh— I'm Claire. I met Garret and Anna at the store—and your husband and son too."

"Oh, that's wonderful." Louise reached for Claire's coat. "And they must've convinced you to join us for lunch then."

"Yes. Anna wouldn't have it any other way."

"Well, good for Anna." Louise hung up Claire's coat, then turned to face her. "You seemed a little upset earlier. Is everything okay?"

Claire saw how Louise's eyes were almost identical to Garret's, same mixture of blue, green, and gray. Why hadn't she noticed this earlier? Perhaps she would have saved herself from a lot of unnecessary upheaval. She sighed deeply. "Can I be perfectly frank with you?"

Louise placed her hand on Claire's. "Of course, please do."

And so Claire began to pour out her story, explaining how she'd first met Garret and Anna on that snowy day, her confusing feelings afterwards, and then how her hopes had risen when they appeared at her showing. Finally she told about her challenge from Jeannie to come back here. "And now I feel like such a fool; I mean I totally lost it when I thought you were Garret's wife. I feel so stupid. And, believe it or not, it's not really like me to do something like—like this."

Louise put her hand over her mouth as if to suppress laughter. "Oh, this is just too incredible!"

Claire stared at her in horror. Did Louise think she was lying? Or perhaps something else? Something worse? "What is it?" she said quietly, preparing herself for the worst. "What's wrong?"

Louise waved her hand. "I'm sorry, Claire; forgive me. But, you see, Garret called me a week or so ago. He told me all about how this beautiful artist appeared on his porch in the middle of a blizzard one day. At first he made it sound like it was only Anna who'd been so taken in by you, but I could tell right away that his heart was involved. But then he said that he noticed you were wearing a wedding ring and so, he figured, erroneously as it turns out, that that was that. Then just a couple days later, Lucy, you know, down at the store, straightened him out on that account. And then he and Anna made that special trip just to see you at your opening. And, well, my poor brother's been wracking his brain trying to figure out a way to get together with you ever since."

"Really?"

Louise nodded with girlish enthusiasm. "Just don't say you heard it from me." She glanced out the window toward the driveway. "And one more thing before they get back: Garret's wife died of cancer about six years ago. It was very unexpected and tragic. He's never really had a serious relationship since then."

Claire swallowed. "Thanks for telling me all this."

"Well, I don't want to overwhelm you, but I don't want you running back off to the city prematurely either."

Claire smiled. "I guess maybe I could stick around a bit longer."

Louise squeezed her hand. "Good."

"Can I give you a hand with anything?" Claire glanced around the room, longing for something to do, something to keep her busy and distract her thoughts. "I heard you're a whiz in the kitchen, but I'd love to help."

"Sure, why don't you make the salad?"

Claire focused all her attention on cleaning and cutting and prettily arranging the salad ingredients into the big wooden bowl, and by the time she heard the front door opening, she thought maybe she could handle this. Just maybe.

17

Anna shrieked when she walked in the front door, causing both Louise and Claire to drop what they were doing and dash out of the kitchen just in time to see the girl staring at the painting that was now propped on a chair.

"Is this *it?*" Anna cried. "Claire, did you really bring this for me?"

Claire nodded. "I thought you should have it."

Anna shook her head. "I cannot believe it. This is so cool!"

"Are you sure about this?" asked Garret, his eyes concerned. "This is a very valuable—"

"I want her to have it." Claire folded her arms across her chest in what she hoped appeared to be a convincing posture but was merely an attempt to conceal her now trembling hands.

"It's very generous." Garret turned to Doug. "Come here, you've got to see this." Then he began telling Doug about Claire's showing in the city. Claire felt certain she could hear the pride in Garret's voice, and she turned away, hiding her pleased smile. The two men stood with Anna, admiring the painting.

Louise and Claire had barely returned to their final preparations in the kitchen before the elderly Hendersons arrived, and suddenly the little cabin was overflowing with laughter and voices. If the couple felt surprised to discover an unexpected guest, they didn't show it. Before long Claire felt almost like part of the family. She laughed as young Hayden galloped through the kitchen, chasing after Michael, who was having the time of his life.

Claire was beginning to feel more relaxed now, and lunch went relatively smoothly. The interesting mix of people and ages kept the conversation hopping from one topic to the next—a great relief to Claire since she already felt like she'd hopped onto a roller coaster today. She kept herself from looking at Garret too often, afraid that others at the table might notice and wonder, or that she might make him feel uncomfortable. But she did sneak an occasional quick peek, at the same time wanting to pinch herself, wondering if all that Louise had told her could possibly be true.

Finally, she felt it was time for her to leave. "Thanks so much," she said, getting up from the table. "It was so nice to meet everyone, and lunch was delicious. I'm glad Anna talked me into it. But I really should hit the road—"

"You're not thinking about going back to the city today, are you?" Louise's question sounded innocent enough, but Claire could tell by the glint in her eyes that she was up to something. "You don't really want to be making that long trip back to San Francisco on Christmas Eve, do you?"

"Well, I—"

"We're all going out to cut a tree this afternoon," Louise continued. "Can't you stay a little longer and go with us?"

"Oh, please," begged Anna. "Come get a tree with us, *please?*"

"It's quite an experience," said Garret. "Tree hunting with the Hendersons. Why, it might even inspire you to paint something . . . comical."

She smiled. "Well, I suppose I could stay a little longer." She glanced over to Michael who was now stretched contentedly by the fire. "And I know my dog's not all that eager to get back to the city." She laughed. "In fact, if I didn't know better, I might think he actually planned this whole thing by getting himself lost today."

"God does work in mysterious ways." Louise grinned.

"I better go back to the cabin first." Claire thought for a moment. "I need to change into hiking clothes, and if I'm staying the night, I'll need to get the fire going again— it's my only source of heat there."

Anna's eyes were bright. "Then you'll come back and join us?"

Claire smiled. "I guess so."

Garret walked her out to the driveway. "I'm glad you're going to stick around, Claire." He opened her door for her. "I was a little worried earlier. I mean you didn't seem all that glad to see us up at the store. I thought maybe I'd done something to offend you."

She shook her head. "Oh, no. I was just feeling a little rattled, I guess. You know, being in a hurry and losing

Michael and all." She had no intention of telling him that she'd been upset because she'd assumed Louise was his wife.

"I'd really been hoping—actually praying even—for the chance to get better acquainted with you. It's occurred to me more than once how I might've come across as, well, a little unfriendly that day you were here at the cabin."

She shrugged. "Oh, I just figured you were absorbed with your writing. I know how it goes; I can be like that with my art sometimes."

"That wasn't really it though." He looked down at her left hand, then exhaled slowly as if he were about to say something he was unsure of. "I—I noticed you wear a wedding ring. . . ."

She looked down at her ring, watched as the diamond glistened in the sun. Why *hadn't* she removed it yet, tucked it safely away, before she returned to the mountains? Was it simply because she'd been in such a hurry, or was it something else? She looked back at Garret.

"Lucy told me that you'd lost your husband and son." He squinted up toward the sky now, pausing uncomfortably. "And I suppose it's possible, maybe even likely, that you're not really ready for—" He stopped himself, running his hand through his hair nervously. Then he shook his head and sighed, as if it were hopeless.

She attempted a weak smile. "It's okay, I think I understand." She looked into his eyes now. "I'm glad that Lucy told you about it. It's true, my husband and son were drowned—it was a boating accident—about eighteen months ago."

"I'm sorry."

"It's been a long hard process for me, getting through the loss, I mean. But coming up here to the mountains was a real breakthrough. And I honestly think I've finally let them go." She looked down at her ring. "I'm so used to wearing this that I didn't even think to take it off. I guess I should."

"I know how you feel. Despite what people tell you, it's never easy to move on. But I do think it gets better with time."

"Yeah, and I feel like I've had some good help along the way."

He nodded. "We can't do it without help."

She studied him carefully, then surprised herself by her next question. "Do you believe in angels, Garret?"

The corners of his lips curved up just slightly. "Yeah, as a matter of fact, I do."

She sighed. "Good."

"So, you're going to stick around then? I haven't completely scared you off?"

She smiled. "I don't really scare that easily." Then she remembered something. "You know, I'd been thinking if I stayed here and was alone for Christmas, I was going to invite Lucy over—she's alone for the holidays and—"

"Of course, she can come spend the holidays with all of us!" exclaimed Garret. "I don't know why I didn't think of it sooner. She and Mom are old friends."

And so it was settled.

Claire spent most of her time during the holidays with the Hendersons. They included both her and Lucy in almost everything, doing all they could to make them both feel completely at home—like one of them—part of the family. It was a Christmas Claire would never forget.

The day after Christmas, Anna and Garret invited her to take a walk with them. She had expressed curiosity about their walking route, not mentioning how it had coincided with her own and perhaps even initiated this whole amazing turn of events right from the beginning. They started out from the Henderson cabin and followed a trail that cut through a thickly wooded area and emerged right along the other side of the dead tree—now she could easily see how the two paths converged. Anna and Michael happily led the way with Claire and Garret lagging just slightly behind. As they came to the bridge, Claire told Garret the meaning of the footprints in the snow. She explained how she'd been haunted by them at first, inspired by them later, and finally how she was driven to follow them in an effort to put her mind at peace. She told him of her frenzied chase through the blinding snowstorm and how she still had no earthly idea how she'd ever made it safely to his cabin.

"Incredible." He shook his head in amazement.

"I know. It's almost unbelievable."

"But did you say that you actually *saw* our footprints on *that* day?" he asked, an odd expression on his face. "The day you got lost and wound up on our porch?"

"Yes. They were nice and clear to start out with. You know how we'd just had a few inches of fresh snow the night before? So, in the beginning the footprints were quite easy to follow, until it started snowing, that is."

He stopped walking and turned to face her, intently studying her, his hand gently resting on her shoulder. "But,

Claire," he said slowly. "We *didn't* take a walk that day. In fact, Anna had been rather upset with me because we hadn't gone out for a walk for several days—I'd been too absorbed in my writing."

"But they were there." Claire stared up into his eyes, unsure as to why he would question her on something like this. "Honest, the footprints were there. I'm not making this up!"

He nodded. "Oh, I believe you."

"But you said you two hadn't walked—"

"That's right. We hadn't. But I have no doubt that you saw footprints that day. They just didn't belong to Anna and me."

She considered his words for a moment. "Are you saying . . . ?"

He pushed a stray curl from her eyes and smiled. "I already told you, Claire, I really do believe in angels."

Melody Carlson is the prolific author of over 70 books of fiction, non-fiction, and gift books for adults, young adults, and children. Her most recent novel is *Blood Sisters* (Harvest House 2001), and she is currently on top for writing *The Prayer of Jabez for Kids* with Bruce Wilkinson for Tommy Nelson. Her writing has won several Rita awards, including a Gold Medallion for *King of the Stable* (Crossway 1998) and a Romance Writers of America Rita award for *Homeward* (Multnomah 1997). She lives with her husband in Sisters, Oregon.